Seeds
of
Liberty

America ❧ France ❧ Ireland

Three Battles for Independence

CLAIRE HENNESSY

Published 2014
by Poolbeg Press Ltd
123 Grange Hill, Baldoyle
Dublin 13, Ireland
E-mail: poolbeg@poolbeg.com

Typesetting, layout, design, ebook © Poolbeg Press Ltd.

1

A catalogue record for this book is available from the British Library.

ISBN 978-1-78199-973-8

Typeset by Poolbeg

Cover illustrated by Derry Dillon

Printed by CPI Group (UK) Ltd, Croydon, CR0 4YY

www.poolbeg.com

About the Author

Claire Hennessy spends most of her time in her own head. Sometimes she writes things down. She is the author of several novels for teenagers, and also teaches creative writing workshops to all ages. At college she studied history and literature (lots of reading, lots of learning, lots of imagining). She lives in Dublin, and also online at *www.clairehennessy.com*. She likes tea and chocolate. A lot.

America

Boston, 1770

16th January

It is bitterly cold outside and I can't sleep. It's my job to make sure the fires don't go out. We lit them this evening to keep everyone in the tavern warm but, even though everyone's gone home now and they've died down, we still need the embers to keep us warm so we don't freeze in our beds. There was a time just before Christmas when we had to start up a fire all over again and Aunt Charlotte was furious with me. But she often is, so I didn't pay her too much heed.

The truth is I wouldn't mind too much if I woke up tomorrow morning and me and Sarah were the only two left alive.

18th January

I need to make sure I hide this book in case Aunt Charlotte or Uncle Alexander or Grandma finds it. They'd most likely whip me for thinking wicked things. Whenever Grandma looks at me I can tell she's thinking I'm a wicked boy. "Jack, have you been thieving?" she asked me yesterday when she saw me with a shining coin. One of the merchants who often comes into the tavern gave it to me for delivering a message across town. I told her that, and she didn't believe me. Then she wanted to know if I'd been "neglecting my duties" here in order to run messages for someone else.

She is impossible to please! She thinks she is so pious and good, but I think she is rotten.

I really must hide this book.

1st February

Sarah is eight today. I asked Aunt Charlotte if this meant she was old enough to take over my job of emptying the chamber pots, and she just laughed. (Grandma scowled and said I was "a wretched lazy boy who didn't know how lucky he was".) I didn't mean to be funny but it's probably best Aunt Charlotte took it that way instead of smacking me.

When I was younger, seven or eight, I asked Aunt Charlotte why I had to empty the chamber pots and she said, "Someone has to do it, Jack". And when I wanted to know why someone else couldn't do it she said that I was just the right age and it was important for me to "know my place". So I thought maybe now that Sarah's just that age things might change, and maybe I'd be allowed do the things our cousin William gets to do. But now that I think about it, most of what William does is tell me what to do – to fetch this, or to clean that. And there's no one younger for me to boss around like that, except Sarah, and I couldn't do that. I'd feel awful. For one thing she's a girl, and she has fair hair and big blue eyes that make her look so innocent and angelic, even if she's misbehaving. And for another she's my sister and the only sister I have, so it's my job to make sure she's being looked after.

That's what our mother said before she died. Sarah doesn't remember much about her, but I do. Sarah was only three but I was five and I remember the way she'd sing to us before we went to sleep, and the stories she'd tell about when she was a girl. She told us about our father, a brave soldier who died in the war, back when the British – us colonists here and all the troops they sent in from across the sea – were fighting against the French. She used to tell me I'd grow up to be handsome and strong just like him. Now that I'm ten I'm not sure I believe that but I like that she said it. And the most important thing she said was that I had to look out for Sarah if anything happened to her.

Or *when* it happened to her. I don't remember when

she started changing the way she talked about it but I guess she knew she was sick for a long time. I didn't really understand then. I was too little. She sent word to Uncle Alexander, her older brother, and after she died he and Aunt Charlotte took us in.

It was all miserable back then, because we were sad about our mother and Aunt Charlotte had just had a baby who hadn't survived the winter and Grandma just kept saying about how it was God's will and we should all pray for strength, which didn't really do anyone much good. And me and Sarah – well, we just wanted to be back home. We didn't understand that we couldn't ever go back, or that she was really gone forever. Forever's an awful long time. No one really tells you that. Maybe you only learn it when someone you love dies.

2nd February

Last night Sarah sneaked out of bed – she shares with Grandma, who is a light sleeper, so she always has to be careful about making noise – and wanted me to tell her some of the stories our mother used to tell us. I'm still yawning this morning but I couldn't say no to her, and anyway it was her birthday. I had nothing else to give her. When Aunt Charlotte found out about the money the merchant had given me, she made me give it to her to help with our keep. I didn't want to hand it over but I suppose she's right. They've taken us in and they didn't have to, and times are tough now. I don't exactly understand everything but it's to do with all the British troops in their red coats that have been in Boston these past few years, and the taxes that the British government over the sea are putting on things.

The men in the red coats have strange accents, all different sorts. Some sound like they have marbles in their mouths and others sound like they're singing all the time. One of those singing sorts came into the tavern recently and I asked where he was from. He said Wales, which sounded at first like "whales" in my head and I thought he might be like those children in stories who are raised by wild animals, like wolves. But it is part of Britain, and beautiful, he told me. "Do you miss it?" I wanted to know. He nodded. It's strange to think of a big strong man with a uniform and musket – he called his "Brown Bess" – as missing home. It made me feel better about sometimes wishing that I could take Sarah and run away to our old house, even though it was more cramped than where we live now. I know it wouldn't be the same and it's not going to bring our mother back but sometimes, especially when Sarah wants the stories, it's hard not to wish for the impossible.

8th February
Uncle Alexander got into an argument with someone today about importing British goods – I think the man

was trying to slyly accuse him of being an importer, which is not approved of these days. People say: "No taxation without representation." Mr Otis, who is a lawyer in the town, says it's "tyranny", what the British are doing. The government put taxes on things that affect us in the colonies, but no one in any of the colonies – there are thirteen, but I've never been outside of Massachusetts, that I can remember anyway – gets to vote for the men that go into government. So I suppose it isn't fair, but who's to say that the men that people like Uncle Alexander would vote in wouldn't do exactly the same thing?

At any rate, the man finally said that Uncle Alexander was probably "more of a Whig than a Tory". I'd heard the words before but didn't really understand them, so I asked William what they meant – which was a bad idea. If I'd thought about it before I opened my mouth I probably would have decided it was worth being kept in suspense and staying curious for another while longer, instead of being treated to one of his superior looks and that way he shakes his head as though I don't know *anything*.

"You really are a simpleton," he said. It's not the first time he's said this but he never says it when Aunt Charlotte is around, so I don't think it's true. I can write and read and do arithmetic and lots of other things, but William is older than me, fifteen on his next birthday, and always seems to know what's going on and what everything means. Like Whigs and Tories.

It occurs to me now, writing this, that I should have said, "I bet you don't know what they mean either, you're just pretending." That would have made him determined to tell me straight away. Instead he said a lot of things about how it was not really any of my business and I was only a boy and I couldn't possibly understand, but that it was to do with the different groups in the British parliament and what they wanted. The Tories think that King George should be able to tell us what to do and the Whigs are on the side of the patriots, which is the name for people who say things like "No taxation without representation" and think that people here should be allowed to decide taxes for themselves.

"What are you, then? A Whig or a Tory?" I asked.

He scoffed. "Nothing yet. I'm waiting to see who wins."

The way he said it makes it sound like there's going to be a fight of some kind.

20th February

I was running errands today, mostly delivering messages (I think overdue bills) for Uncle Alexander, when the matter of importing came up again among some of the boys I met along the way. There are a few I know well enough to talk to, though not so much that

I'd trust them with my life if it ever came to it. There's one, Daniel, an apprentice to a tailor who lives nearby, who is especially good-natured – he must be about William's age but he would never look at me the way William does. Today he told me that there are still merchants in Boston who are importing British goods, or selling to the British, and that the patriots are not happy about it. He made the patriots' attitude seem much more sensible. If everyone decides that the taxes are wrong, and everyone stands together, then things will have to change. But if some people sneak around, it ruins it for everyone.

22nd February

An awful thing has happened. I didn't mean to get caught up in anything, but Uncle Alexander has beaten me anyway. Every bit of me aches. He says I deserve it.

I was just on my way back to the tavern when I saw Daniel and some of the others, talking and laughing and excited. They were on their way to one of the shops that is still importing goods, and yelled at me to come and join them. I suppose I got caught up in the fun of it. I don't know if I am a patriot the way Daniel seems to be, especially after what happened today, but when the boys were talking it did seem to matter fiercely, all of this business. So I went with them to the shop in the North End. It had a sign up saying

"Importer" and there were already a number of men outside shouting things at the customers.

A man came along to take down the sign and someone yelled that he was a customs informer and then other people shouted worse things at him, and suddenly we were chasing him down the street and throwing whatever we could find at him – clumps of dirt, mostly, and sticks.

We chased him back to his own house and Daniel said, "We'll teach him a lesson." He was smiling as he said it. It's difficult not to trust someone who smiles like that, even if their next move is to pick up a stone and hurl it at someone's house.

Other people were doing the same thing, and then out through one of the broken windows the customs man opened fire. That put an end to things. At least one boy, Christopher, who can't be much older than me, was shot – I hope the people taking care of him are doing their best to make sure he recovers. There was an awful lot of blood but Daniel said lots of people get shot and survive. He wasn't smiling, though.

At any rate, Uncle Alexander is disgusted that I took part in "that patriot nonsense" and says that, if we behave in such a way, no wonder the British parliament think they need to make all our laws. We can't be trusted to govern ourselves.

My eyes are starting to grow tired and the candlelight is barely enough to write by, but writing this stops me thinking about all the bruises and the marks left by the beating.

23rd February

Sometimes little sisters are not the worst. Sarah crept out of bed last night to sneak me some food – I hadn't been given any dinner, on account of my "misbehaviour", but I had managed to already sneak some myself. Still, it was a kind thing for her to do, especially since Uncle Alexander had said quite firmly that she wasn't to talk to me last night and was particularly strict about sending me to bed with an empty stomach.

24th February

Daniel just told me the news. Christopher, the boy who was shot that day, died that night. Samuel Adams, who is one of the town leaders and a patriot, is arranging the funeral.

25th February

When Uncle Alexander heard that one of the boys had died, he said, "Serves him right" and gave me a long lecture about the importance of behaving myself and not getting caught up in scuffles and scrapes. "Otherwise," he said, "you'll end up the same way."

"Don't frighten the boy," Aunt Charlotte said. "He's learned his lesson."

"Ha!" Grandma said. "That one never learns."

I felt as though I was invisible. They were talking about me but not to me, which happens often, but felt more unfair this time.

I kept thinking about poor Christopher and then I wondered if he had a little sister who might have counted on him.

27th February

The funeral took place yesterday and there were scores of people there, which is at least something. So many people are furious that someone so young and innocent has died in this way – "murdered", some say, or "slaughtered", which are strong words but seem to fit the awfulness of it. The procession began at the Liberty Tree, where patriots gather, and they will put up a sign there and are talking about a monument so that everyone remembers what happened. There were so many people weeping, whether they knew him or not, talking about how awful it is that an innocent child had to die.

It was very different from my mother's funeral and even though I am sad about Christopher, I found myself thinking about her.

Sarah came to the funeral with me but she didn't cry. She was very quiet the whole time. Aunt Charlotte said we were allowed to go, but that she wasn't going to accompany us because Uncle Alexander was still furious about it all. In conversations with other people he has said it is a tragedy, but I know he still thinks that boys who throw rocks at the officials are asking for trouble.

4th March

There was a fight on Saturday between some soldiers and workers at John Gray's ropewalks – Daniel says the soldiers started it, Uncle Alexander says the workers started it. I don't know who's telling the truth and I don't think either of them really know – they weren't there. The workers there are likely to shout out something that might offend a soldier, but then again the redcoats are sometimes quite rude. I hope the man from Wales wasn't involved. I can't imagine him getting into a fight just for the sake of it.

5th March

I think I can hear bells ringing – perhaps there's a fire somewhere. I am so tired I just want to curl up and sleep, but Aunt Charlotte insists I work in the tavern this evening and not be a lazy layabout.

My bruises have mostly vanished now. I almost miss watching them change colours.

6th March

There was trouble outside the Customs House last night – that was what the bells were, I think. A crowd gathered there and then the redcoats – or as Daniel calls them, "lobsterbacks" – started firing when the crowd wouldn't go away. It started out with someone talking about a British officer not paying a bill he owed, and then the soldier got annoyed about what was being said about the troops and hit the man. That's what Daniel heard anyway – he came into the tavern today and told me all about it. He and one or two other boys joined the crowd around this point and the soldier who started it called in more troops, and then there were lots of soldiers there who said they wouldn't fire, that they were just trying to keep order.

"And then what did the damn lobsterbacks do?" Daniel said to me, his fists clenched.

The answer was obvious, but I don't think it was the sort of question he expected me to answer. They opened fire, of course, and killed at least three men instantly. An apprentice that Daniel knew, Sam, died early this morning from his wounds.

Just as Daniel was telling me this, Aunt Charlotte came over to us with a stern look on her face and wanted to know if Daniel's master knew he was skiving off work in the middle of the day to drink in her tavern.

If she had said something like that to me I would have immediately felt the need to explain or to apologise, but Daniel looked at her and said, "Today is a day of mourning, Mrs Young." He sounded so grown-up and wise, like he was her equal, and to her credit she nodded as if to say, 'Well, that's all right then'.

"It's a terrible loss for all of Boston, what happened last night," she said. But then she added, "I hope you weren't caught up in it, Daniel."

He had the sense to deny this.

When she was gone, he said, "I'm not ashamed of being a patriot, Jack. But I don't want to get you into any trouble."

"You won't," I said, even though that's not entirely true. If Aunt Charlotte knew he had been out with those men last night she would probably tell Uncle Alexander and then it'd be another beating for me. This way, though, she let me stay talking to him a bit longer and he got to talk more about Sam. I think he needed someone to listen to him. It must be awful to have a friend be killed. I wonder does it feel different if someone is killed by other people instead of by a sickness?

12th March

People are still talking about the "horrid massacre". Even Uncle Alexander is furious about it. He said that even though people should have known better than to pick a fight with the troops, the soldiers had no right to open fire like that. "They surely weren't given the order to fire," he said. "If there's no discipline in the army then what right do they have disciplining anyone else?"

A group of gentlemen were picked by the townspeople to ask the governor to send away the troops, saying that unless they were removed there would only be more bloodshed. They have been moved out of the city for now. There are calls for them to be tried for murder too.

The funeral procession for the four men who died took place last Thursday evening. The entire town ground to a halt – we closed the tavern, and most of the shops were shut too. Everyone was very solemn and sad, and I saw someone who could only be Sam's mother, looking so heartbroken it made me want to turn away immediately.

Aunt Charlotte was dabbing her eyes with a handkerchief. "She's a widow, you know," she whispered. "The poor woman, without even a husband to comfort her . . ." Even as she said this, Uncle Alexander was turned away from her, so the idea of husbands being there for comforting their wives seemed pretty funny, but I knew I mustn't laugh.

Sarah was quiet again, like she was at Christopher's funeral, but no one else seemed to notice or mind much. I suppose at funerals everyone's supposed to be quiet, but I could tell it meant something was going on behind those big blue eyes. Sure enough, the next night I woke up to find her tugging at my sleeve.

Sometimes I think about how Uncle Alexander was

our mother's older brother and I wonder if she ever woke him up in the middle of the night because she wanted to be told a story or she was scared and there was no one else she trusted. It isn't really the sort of thing I can ask him, not least because he might beat Sarah for being out of bed so often.

At any rate, Sarah wanted to know if the redcoats were going to kill everyone. She said "everyone" but really what she was asking was if they were going to kill *her*.

"Don't worry," I said. "They're not going to shoot you." That much I do believe. She's just a little girl, and I don't think even the most cold-hearted lobsterback would hurt her.

"What about you?" She was sobbing by that stage, but I put my hand over her mouth and stroked her hair a little bit to try to get her to stop. Otherwise she'd wake someone up.

"They're not going to shoot me," I said, but even as I said it a cold feeling came over me.

We did this for everyone in the family and everyone Sarah could think of, every single name, until she started looking like she might be about to drop off to sleep. I began to feel as though I was lying to her. The cold feeling didn't go away until the next morning.

3rd April

People are still talking about the massacre, and there

are prints being sold of an engraving that shows how it happened, made by Paul Revere, the silversmith and patriot. More and more people seem to be patriots ever since 'The Bloody Massacre'. That's what the title of the engraving is and it is bloody – it shows all the redcoats lined up and firing on one side, and the crowd on the other, bleeding and wounded and even holding their hands up to say stop.

There are loyalists – Tories – in the town who say these are all lies and that the troops were victims of the dangerous patriots, and there are so many different stories about it I don't know what to think. But five people so far have died because of that day – another man died of his injuries a fortnight ago and perhaps another still might, he is crippled at any rate – and not a single one was a soldier in the king's troops.

28th April

The trials of the soldiers have not yet taken place. I saw Daniel today for the first time in a few weeks and he spoke about it. It had faded from my mind a little bit. Grandma has been ill and demanded I sit with her and read to her from the Bible. I don't understand why she needed me to do this, because every time I stumbled over a word or missed a line she was ready to correct me, so she must know the whole thing by heart. There are some good stories in there, I'll grant you, but I wished she'd choose another book, especially as the words were so small and my eyes grew sore trying to make them out. I asked several times if she wouldn't rather William read to her but she scoffed and told me to get on with it.

Sarah suggested that perhaps she likes my voice but I think Grandma was just hoping that all the Bible reading would make a good impression on me.

15th June
Since the last time I wrote in here I have had a birthday. I am now eleven, and still not yet handsome and strong like my father was.

My reading is getting better, though. I don't get caught on words so much any more, if that counts for anything.

The British parliament have decided to get rid of some of the taxes on goods but are still taxing other things, like tea. I wonder how they decide what to tax and if it has anything to do with what they all like to drink in the mornings.

24th September
William is in a temper again. He's been like this for the past few months. Sometimes he's really cheerful and then other times he's very grumpy I think it's to do with the girl he's been courting. Today she must have done or said something that rubbed him up the wrong way because he's been stomping around the place and

ordering me around even more than usual.

Uncle Alexander thinks the "non-importation movement" will have to come to an end here. It already stopped in New York a few months ago, and Philadelphia have just followed suit, he says. I suppose we will be serving British tea again soon.

I can still hear William shouting at someone – oh, Uncle Alexander. He's raising his voice too.

I wish Daniel was my brother instead of William. A whole bunch of us had some great fun over the summer, swimming and playing games, but now it's getting colder already and there's so much more work to be done.

Boston, 1771

6th March

For a while there I didn't feel like writing much in this book. Sometimes in the tavern all the days melt together.

Yesterday we all went to a speech by Mr Lovell. He teaches at the Latin School, where William used to go for a bit but didn't finish. Really, boys only stay on there if they're going to go on to college and William knows he's going to inherit his father's business so there's no need. Anyway, Mr Lovell spoke about the massacre last year, because it's one year since it happened, and it was very solemn but he also talked about how you shouldn't have an army there if it's peacetime, which seemed to make sense.

The trials of the soldiers took place last winter, finally. Daniel talked a lot about it when it was happening. He's still furious about it. They tried the captain first and then he was let off because they found he hadn't given the order to fire, just like Uncle Alexander said, so it seemed then more likely that the soldiers were guilty. Because they'd just decided to start shooting instead of waiting for an order.

"They hate us," Daniel kept saying. He seemed so gloomy about it so much of the time, but then his face would light up and he'd say things like, "But they'll hang for it!" or else change the subject entirely.

There were eight soldiers on trial and most of them were acquitted – I think that's the word I mean. They were let off the hook. Two of them were found guilty of firing on the crowd and killing those men but because they were "provoked" it was said to be manslaughter and not murder, and then they pleaded for leniency and only ended up branded instead of hanged for it.

Daniel and a lot of the other patriots in the town were bitterly disappointed about this. And there were men who call themselves patriots who defended the soldiers – Mr Quincy and Mr Adams (John, not Samuel – there are two important men in the town called Mr Adams – I think they are cousins).

A lot of people just wanted to see the soldiers hanged and certainly not defended, but Uncle

Alexander approved of what happened. He said it showed that Boston was a civilised place. He thinks it will prove something to the British.

I don't know about that, but after Mr Lovell's speech last night there seemed to be a lot of people who were still very annoyed about the British and the things we don't get a say in.

17th June

Grandma is ill again. This time Sarah has been tending to her, which is a relief. Aunt Charlotte thinks girls need to know more than boys how to care for the sick, except if it's very serious and then the doctor is called in. She says Sarah makes a good nurse.

Sarah is grumpy about it. "She keeps calling me Margaret," she said to me yesterday. "She doesn't know who I am. It's awful." She let out a heavy sigh.

I am ashamed to say that it took me a minute or two to realise what was happening. Our mother's name was Margaret. And Sarah does look like her, I suppose. But to think that Grandma has forgotten that her own daughter has been dead for several years, and is mixing her up with her granddaughter! I *never* want to grow old if this is how addled the mind gets.

"And then," Sarah continued, in a whisper, "she said I needed to stay away from that dreadful boy."

I grew quite cross. "She never even gives me a chance!" I said. I was all ready to fly into a temper and

25

list all of my grievances (a word Daniel uses – it means the same as complaints but I like the sound of it) with Grandma, but Sarah patted my arm and stopped me.

"I don't think she meant you," she said. "Her mind's all confused. She told me not to *marry* the boy."

Grandma must think it's years ago, when our mother was young. She must mean she didn't want her to marry our father.

9th July

The doctor came to let blood from Grandma. For a time she seemed to be getting better but then she slipped back into feverish ramblings.

"I feel terrible," Sarah told me. "I don't want her to die."

I didn't know what to say. She's old and sick and she may well die. And she's never liked me all that much anyway. I said that last part to Sarah.

"She's never liked me all that much either," she said, sniffling. "But I still don't want her to . . ."

Even William is sad. I caught him crying last week and then he threatened to beat me if I told anyone. Writing it in here doesn't count, I'm sure. At first I thought it might be his girl, but later I saw them together and she looked like she was being kind to him, her face all softened like she thought he was the greatest boy in the whole wide world, so it must have been Grandma. His girl's name is Abigail and her father's a printer, and if they do end up getting married I suppose William might take over the printing business and then Uncle Alexander would have to find someone else to take care of the tavern.

Sometimes I think about what it'd be like to have my own business or a trade, especially to have a father who'd be able to teach you everything you needed to know. Maybe I'll be apprenticed to someone like Daniel is. It's hard work but once you're all trained up you can make a life for yourself.

13th July

After the last time I wrote in here I was so worked up about trades and professions that I asked Aunt Charlotte about becoming a doctor – only because the doctor had just been – and she laughed a little but then tried to cover it up and said kindly that it wasn't the sort of work boys like me did.

I suppose it's work that the boys who go to the Latin School might end up doing. Not boys who leave school once they can read and write.

I wanted to tell Daniel but then I thought he might laugh too, so I told Sarah. She thought about it for a minute and then said, "But you don't want to be a doctor, do you?"

I shrugged.

"If you were a doctor, you'd have to try to make everyone better, even the nasty people," she said.

"So?"

"You'd only save the nice people," she said.

I didn't like the sound of that. It sounded like something Grandma might say, like I was no good.

16th July

I wanted to stay angry with Sarah but Grandma has gone and died so I can't be.

22nd July

The last time I wrote in here I was so angry I can see it in the handwriting. It's all spiky. That's sort of how I've been feeling. Then I lost my temper with William one day and he hit me, and we got into a fight, and both ended up with black eyes. Uncle Alexander was furious with me for losing my temper and furious with William for hitting me – after all, he is bigger and older than me. And he is furious, I suppose, because his mother just died, and even though he's a grown man it must still make someone sad if their mother dies.

Sarah has been praying an awful lot. I haven't, not one bit. At the funeral I only mouthed the words and didn't really say them. That's probably a sin.

I'm not sad that she's died. I know that's a sin.

But I wish she had stayed alive to tell me what she really meant about our father. That's what I wish. I wish I could march in there right now and demand to know why she didn't think our father was good enough for our mother. I'd ask if that's why she's never liked us.

19th October

I haven't seen much of Daniel lately. He says he is busy and looks so mysterious when he says it that it's clear he wants someone to ask why. But every time I ask he says, "I can't tell you". I bet some of the other boys, the older ones, know what's going on, but no one is telling me anything.

Boston, 1772

23rd January

William's Abigail has married someone else! From what people say, her father had a lot to do with this, for her new husband is much older than she is – and he has plenty of money.

I worried that William might turn violent again but instead he has been lounging about and writing *poetry* about her. Whenever Uncle Alexander or Aunt Charlotte sees this, they sigh and tell him to go and be useful, but Sarah listens to him talk about how much he loves Abigail and how beautiful she is and what a wonderful wife she would have made him and how much he hates this man who's come along from New York to steal her away.

"You shouldn't listen to him," I told her, because Sarah is far too young to think about love and marriage. For that matter so am I, and I would just as soon not think about any of it, but it is difficult when William talks of nothing else.

Clearly girls are more trouble than they are worth.

14th April

People seem to be less angry about the British these days. There are still men like Samuel Adams writing about colonists' rights but trade is going well for most people.

But there is a society that still meets called the Sons of Liberty – they are a group of patriots that has existed since the Stamp Act in 1765 which was more 'taxation without representation' on the part of the British Crown, putting a tax on paper for things like wills and newspapers. That Act caused huge protests and the British had to repeal it in the end. Daniel finally told me he is one of the Sons of Liberty, which is why he's been so mysterious. I suppose I hadn't ever thought about it before, but I had heard of the Sons of Liberty and I thought most patriots were probably part of this group. Daniel says some of the patriots want to be careful and not associate with the society officially but they still write pamphlets and have their voices heard.

He thinks eventually Massachusetts will rule itself and there will be no interference from Britain at all.

26th June

William has found a new girl to pine over. This one is the daughter of a shoemaker and is called Martha. She laughs a lot but she has a very ugly face. I said as much to Aunt Charlotte and she hit me.

It is still *true*.

6th November

Sarah thinks we should start our own Committee of Correspondence. There was a meeting last week where one was set up in the town because people are annoyed once more with something the British parliament has decided. It is to do with how judges are paid – it is money from the Crown funds that will pay them now, and that money comes from the taxes we (well, people like Uncle Alexander) pay, but I think people worry about how the judges might be corrupt if this is how they are being paid, instead of being paid by the colony. Sometimes Britain seems very far away, too far to understand how things are here.

Daniel said the Committee is making a list of all the rights we have and then all the grievances people have too, times when these rights have been ignored. I think Sarah thinks they are just all writing letters to one another, but I agreed that we should have our own Committee.

Her first letter says:

Dearest brother, your face is dirty. You look like a chimneysweep!

I am sure the men of the Committee do not send each other messages of this kind.

1st December

I am going to copy out this part of the pamphlet so that I can read it again. The Committee have brought out a publication called 'The Votes and Proceedings of the Freeholders and Other Inhabitants of the Town of Boston, in Town Meeting Assembled', which is a long list of the things they decided. A copy was left behind in the tavern but I fear someone will ask for it back soon, so I am going to write quickly.

"Among the natural rights of the colonists are these: first, a right to life; secondly, to liberty; thirdly to property, together with the right to support and defend them in the best manner they can. These are evident branches of, rather than deductions from, the duty of self-preservation, commonly called the first law of nature.

All men have a right to remain in a state of nature as long as they please. And in case of intolerable oppression, civil or religious, to leave the society they belong to, and enter into another."

There is also a later part that says:

"The natural liberty of man is to be free from any superior power on earth, and not to be under the will or legislative authority of man; but only to have the law of nature for his rule."

I wish I could write more quickly. There are more than forty pages in this pamphlet but I had better return it downstairs, before I get into trouble for thieving instead of what I was really doing, which was borrowing.

3rd December

"A right to life" I can understand. Unless someone commits a crime and pays for it with their life. A right to "liberty" seems much bigger and not really true. Otherwise I would be able to do what I like instead of being told by Uncle Alexander or Aunt Charlotte or William to clean up this or fetch that. And staying in "a state of nature" sounds like walking around without any clothes on. It is far too cold to do that.

That is probably not what they mean but it made me laugh.

Boston, 1773

22nd January
Sarah and I are still sending each other letters – her handwriting is much better now. Mostly it is about food. We are tired of stew.

It is a cold winter. I suppose they all are but it's funny how easy it is to forget about snow and frost in the middle of the summer, as though they never existed.

15th February
An old school friend of Uncle Alexander's has come to stay with us. He has business in Boston but that's all he ever says, which I imagine probably means he has

meetings with smugglers or the Sons of Liberty or both. His name is Mr Miller and the first thing he said when he saw me was, "Ah, you must be Margaret's boy."

It was such a shock to hear him say that. Aunt Charlotte and Uncle Alexander never say her name. I used to think it was because it made them too sad to think about her, but they still talk about Grandma.

All I could do was nod.

23rd February

I saw Daniel today when I was collecting some goods for Mr Miller from the wharf. He says that pamphlet about liberty and all that has gone around to lots of other towns in Massachusetts and even to some of the other colonies. "More and more men are becoming patriots," he said. "Soon we will have liberty, mark my words." He grinned and clapped me on the back. "And soon you'll be old enough to fight for it, if you have to."

"Fight?" I tried to make myself look a little taller. "Do you think we'll have to?"

Daniel shrugged. "We'll fight with words first. Most people think the British can be made see sense."

"What do you think?"

He leaned in a little closer. "I think we'll have to fight."

"Then we'll fight," I said.

Daniel nodded in approval.

On my way home I thought about how I know nothing about fighting and how I would be of no use if there is a war. I also thought about what we would be fighting for. Liberty. I still don't understand what it means. Freedom from the British parliament but not from the rich people in town? Freedom for some people but not everyone? Will it mean we have more money? I don't know.

I trust Daniel but all my life I have known that, when there is war, people die. My mother always said my father died a hero, a brave soldier, but I am not him.

5th March

The town marked the anniversary again today. A man named Dr Benjamin Church gave the speech this year. He treated some of the wounded that day and he talks very well, but I could hardly concentrate.

Mr Miller has left, but the night before his departure he and Uncle Alexander stayed up late drinking rum and talking about what life was like when they were boys. I had been sent to bed but I could still hear them, so I crept downstairs to listen to what they were saying.

Ever since Mr Miller mentioned my mother I wondered how much he knew about her and about my father and Grandma disapproving of him. It turns out that Mr Miller wanted to marry her and was bitterly disappointed when she ran off with "that good-for-nothing scoundrel".

"Jack looks like him, a little," Uncle Alexander said.

"I can see it. Like Margaret too, though." He was silent for a moment and then said, "The girl's the same. She's like Margaret was at that stage, but I see parts of that rotten fiend . . ."

Mr Miller has never married and he thinks my mother would still be alive if she'd married him.

"I would have given her a good life," he said.

I didn't like the way they were talking about my father. It's no way to talk about a soldier.

And then today, as soon as Dr Church began speaking, I thought about the soldiers that day. And of course my father would have fought for the British, wouldn't he? We are still British citizens, after all, even if we don't have the same rights as those living in Britain, and they were fighting against the French, so . . .

And perhaps that is why they hated him.

10th March
I have been trying to build up the courage to ask Uncle Alexander or Aunt Charlotte about my father, but there is never a good time to ask. I wonder do they think of him when they look at me?

9th April
I wish I had never asked.

14ᵗʰ April

The worst part is that I asked when Sarah was there. If I had just waited until she had run off to write one of her letters or to play with her rag doll, then she wouldn't know about any of this. She could still believe that our father was a brave soldier who died and that he loved us very much. And that he loved our mother very much.

I finally plucked up the nerve to ask Aunt Charlotte about my father and she was silent for a minute before saying, "I suppose you're both old enough now to know the truth."

I thought I knew what was coming. She would tell us about how Grandma had disapproved of him, and she'd talk about Mr Miller and say that he had wanted to marry our mother and that would have been the best for everyone.

I looked at her, and then at Sarah, who was staring at her in a sort of terror, and I had the foolishness to try to reassure her then.

What Aunt Charlotte had to say was much worse. She did tell us about Mr Miller, but then when she started talking about this other man – a smuggler and a thief, a man who made promises he couldn't keep, a man who couldn't be trusted, I got an awful feeling in my gut.

He wasn't a brave soldier. He didn't die in battle. He was a man who should never have married our mother because, just before Sarah was born, he ran away.

"Margaret thought at first he'd come back," Aunt Charlotte said. "We knew he wouldn't. He ran off to some other woman, most likely."

Sarah's eyes filled up with tears. "He didn't want to see me?"

"He was a bad man," Aunt Charlotte said firmly, and then she said something that surprised me. "I don't want either of you to dwell on this. You're good children. You're not to blame for what your father did."

If she had said that – that we were good – before that day it would have lifted me up. She so rarely praises us, especially me. Too much praise makes people vain and arrogant, and pride goes before a fall – everyone knows that. But then it fell on deaf ears.

16th April

Sarah and I had stopped sending each other letters for a few weeks but I found one in my pocket today after dinner. *Where do you think he is? Do you think he thinks about us and wonders what has become of us?*

I know why she wrote it down. Sometimes it is easier to say things on a page.

I don't know where he might be. I can't imagine he would ever come back to Boston. He must know that people would recognise him, and Uncle Alexander would be sure to confront him about how he treated his sister.

I don't think he ever wonders what has become of us, either. He never even met Sarah, not even when she was a baby, and he must have decided I wasn't worth much.

But what I wrote to her, to fold up and hide behind her doll, was this: *I think he is at sea, having marvellous adventures but also thinking often of his children. Right now he is caught in a storm but he is determined to return to Boston as soon as he is able, and to shower them with riches!*

7th July

Sometimes on the streets I look at the different men and wonder would I know my father if I saw him. Would he know me?

I know why our mother lied. She wanted to protect us. I would have lied to Sarah if I could. I understand it. But I don't like it. Not one bit.

15th October

There are ships filled with tea heading this way from Britain and a new law passed. The East India company will be allowed sell it more cheaply than before, but there are still taxes to be paid when it is unloaded – it is as though they thought perhaps no one would notice that there are still duties on the tea. The tea agents here are already being cautioned not to accept the tea when it arrives. This is a chance to protest, the way people did with the Stamp Act in 1765. This is a chance.

Daniel thinks there might be some fighting.

"Good," I said.

29th November
The first ship, the *Dartmouth*, landed at the harbour yesterday. There are already several men, mostly Sons of Liberty, I think, standing guard to make sure it doesn't unload its cargo.

15th December
Now there are three ships.

The cargo can stay there for twenty days; after that the customs officials are allowed to seize it, if it hasn't been unloaded and if the duty hasn't been paid. Tomorrow is the twentieth day for the *Dartmouth*.

There is a plan. I cannot say more in case someone finds this book, and I have not told anyone, even Sarah, but there is a plan.

For the first time in my entire life I feel I have a purpose of some kind, a place to be.

17th December
It is safe to write about it now. Last night there was a huge meeting about what to do about the tea – to see

if the governor would let it return to England, for example, which he had been refusing to permit, or whether the people of Boston needed to take action.

There were a number of us already ready to take action – Daniel and myself and a large number of other boys and men, most of whom I did not know. Daniel told me they were mainly apprentices and journeymen who would not be particularly well known in the town, and we were all disguised anyway – dressed as Mohawk Indians, and we also had coal dust smeared over our hands and faces. "If you don't know who someone is, you can't turn them in," Daniel said, so I tried to keep that in mind and say as little as possible and try not to peer too closely at any faces through the soot.

When we received the signal, we began whooping and yelling and then ran to the wharf. Divided into three groups, we boarded the ships. The captain of our ship was mostly concerned with whether he would be able to bring his ship back to England, not about the tea, but we were under strict orders not to damage the ship or anything else. The tea was the only thing we were allowed throw overboard. "No looting, either," someone said sternly, and everyone kept a watchful eye out for anyone who might be pocketing some for himself. It would have defeated the whole point if we were just thieving. Many of us were carrying tomahawks – partly as a disguise and partly as a tool

– and we used these to break open the chests of tea. It was harder than I thought it would be. We had to hack away and ensure that we had broken the chest and the canvas protecting the tea, and then and only then could we heave it overboard. It took hours to get through the lot of them, and there were many people standing on the shore watching us. There must have been hundreds of chests of tea overall, and all of them were thrown into the harbour, spreading out in the cold water, ruined.

I ache from all the work but it was worth it. I made sure to scrub my face and hands before returning home, and to hide the disguise. Uncle Alexander was too caught up in talking about what had happened to look too closely at me, which is just as well, because this morning Sarah prodded me sharply and told me there was still some coal dust on my neck.

"I must have leaned too close to the fire last night," I said.

She stared at me. "I think you were an Indian last night."

I told her, but I made her swear not to tell anyone else. The town seems to approve of what happened last night, overall, but Uncle Alexander might not approve of me being caught up in it.

It was exciting, though. Hard work, but I feel more alive than I have in months. I feel I could do anything.

Boston, 1774

16th March

There have been a few more things happening these past few weeks – a Tory customs informer clashing with a shoemaker and being dragged through the streets, another shipment of tea emptied out into the harbour. We are standing up for ourselves.

18th May

They are going to close the port! "Can they do that?" I asked Daniel. They can, of course. There is a new governor, Gage, and ships from the British navy are gathering. And there are troops. The lobsterbacks have returned.

22nd July

The British plan is to make everyone in Boston pay for what happened to the tea. There are new laws called the Intolerable Acts – that is the patriot name for them, anyway – which are supposed to restore order to the colony. The local colonial government is now under the control of the British, with judges and sheriffs appointed by the governor instead of by the colonists. The power to bring men to justice is in their hands, not in ours, even though they hardly seem to know what justice is.

Sometimes I can feel my skin crawling with how unfair it is, but I know I'm not alone in this. Even William hates what is happening. Whether it will be enough to make him do something about it, if the time comes, is another thing, but I remember when he only wanted to back the winning side, or to wait and see.

These actions are not bringing order. They're turning people into patriots. And the British will have only themselves to blame.

29th September

Representatives of the different colonies have met in Philadelphia to discuss everything that's been happening. They're trying to make sure everyone agrees to non-importation of British goods so that the parliament will see that they need to stop taxing us without letting us have a say in the matter.

I wonder if it will work. It feels like this has been going on for far too long. Something must change.

13th October

With the port closed it means that we are cut off from most trade, but the other colonies are sending us food. They're on our side.

"What they're doing," Daniel said, meaning the British, "affects everyone. They're trampling all over our rights as colonists. If they don't stop soon . . ."

He didn't need to finish the sentence. I know what he meant.

The local militia units are becoming more serious. Any man over the age of sixteen is supposed to join, and it used to be that they would meet and train perhaps a few times a year, but now it feels as though they are preparing for war. William has taken to it well, and his girl Martha is proud of him. It doesn't seem as though anyone else will marry her so William's chances are good. When I said this to Sarah, she said, "Don't say it in such a way, Jack. She adores him."

"She looks like a pig," I said, which is true. Her nose is squished in that same way. And her laugh is a little like a squeal.

"I think you're jealous that none of the girls of the town will even look at you," she said.

Sarah has always been interested in romance but

lately it has become even worse. She blushes whenever Daniel comes into the tavern or she sees him on the streets, even though she is far too young to even dream of marriage. And she is preoccupied with other people and who they might be in love with. There is a widower who lives a few houses away who she thinks should marry the seamstress whose husband died last year, for example – I think they are both too old to think about such things, never mind to have Sarah inventing fairy tales about them.

Anyway, she's wrong about the girls not looking at me. I know from what some of the boys say that there are girls who would want to be courted by me, but I can't imagine why. It seems so much less important than what is happening right now to us, as colonists, as Americans.

4th November

Martha has agreed to marry William, although her father would prefer she waits until she turns eighteen, so the wedding will not be for another few months. Aunt Charlotte thinks this is very sensible, even though she was married younger than that – I think sixteen.

"She needs to grow up a little more before she becomes a wife and mother," Sarah said, for all the world sounding like a mother herself instead of not yet thirteen.

Meanwhile, in the tavern, I am keeping my ears open for any news about the lobsterbacks or what they might be planning. Being a spy sounds exciting but it isn't really. It's just that men sometimes say things around boys, particularly ones who are just serving their food or drinks, or cleaning up nearby, that they mightn't otherwise say. Whenever there are men who are known loyalists about, my ears are kept pricked up like a dog's, just in case.

21st November

What a day! I am lucky to be alive, not to have been shot with one of those 'Brown Bess' muskets. That's what Daniel told me, and what Aunt Charlotte told me, but even she is so tired of the troops being here that she was worried for my safety instead of chastising me for my insolence.

I had just met with Daniel and some others and had found out that two soldiers had defected from the army and were going into hiding, which was wonderful news. If even their own troops are turning against them, the British can't hope to win. So when I saw the familiar flashes of red at the end of the street, just a few minutes away from home, I was prepared to ignore anything rude they might call after me.

And then I saw that they were talking to two girls, one of whom was Sarah, and I yelled out and started running. I had only just said farewell to Daniel, and he ran after me, but I didn't notice at the time. I had heard stories about how the soldiers treated girls, and had been there at moments when they shouted appallingly crude things at them, and all I could think about was making whatever was happening stop.

"Leave them alone!" I shouted, and one of them laughed.

"We're just talking to these ladies," he said, but there was a look in his eye I didn't like.

Sarah and her friend – I recognised her then as Anne, a cousin of Martha – didn't look like they were having a friendly discussion either. They looked scared.

"Well, you'd best say goodbye now," I said, and then he sneered, and my fist was in his face before I knew what I was doing.

And then the other had his musket pointed right at me and Daniel was pulling me back. "He didn't mean it," he said. "The girl is his sister. Leave him be."

For a moment time stood still and I was sure the lobsterback would fire. I thought about the boy Christopher who died that time, and of how people mourned him. I wondered would they mourn for me in the same way, or if we have grown too weary to grieve in that way any more. I thought about Sarah weeping for me – I knew *she* would, at any rate. I thought about our father finally returning to Boston one day and discovering his son was dead, and perhaps only then regretting leaving us all those years ago.

Daniel kept talking. "It was an accident," he said, "and you don't want to start shooting here." He indicated to the left and the right of him and I realised people were starting to gather around.

The two soldiers exchanged looks and then I was given a sound whack on the head but not shot, and they shouted for everyone to disperse. There was another moment where it seemed as though things might tilt towards another massacre, but Daniel grabbed my arm and told the girls to come too and tugged us around the corner.

"That was foolish," he said. "You're lucky we got out of there."

I realise now I was lucky he was close by.

He muttered some unrepeatable things about the soldiers, and then told the girls to stay out of their way in the future, and insisted on marching the lot of us back home.

He said something else that has stuck with me. "Don't fight them on your own. That's not how we're going to win this, when the fighting starts. We need to stick together. It's the only way we'll beat them."

Boston, 1775

27th February

The word is that British troops have been out mapping the area lately, preparing for what might happen when it all explodes. Rumours fly around the place and it's difficult to know what to believe – we hear things about the countryside and nearby towns that are sometimes true, sometimes not, and they hear the same about us. The troops haven't opened fire yet. Yet. It's only a matter of time. Everyone is preparing.

Meanwhile on the streets there are more small clashes, more moments where it seems as though it's all building towards something big. "I can feel it," I said to Daniel yesterday, and he nodded. He understands. He feels it too. Things can't go on for much longer like this. There are already plans in place for what will happen if the troops move.

14th March
Sometimes when I see soldiers on the streets now I am glad that my father was never one. They seem haughty and out of place, and I long for the day when they vanish entirely from our towns and our colonies.

William and Martha are married now. It was a dull affair, I thought, but they both seemed happy.

19th April
The troops marched out last night towards the towns of Lexington and Concord, we think possibly to arrest some patriots or to seize their stores of military supplies or both. Fortunately, our spies found out what was going on, and some of our alarm riders – Paul Revere, William Dawes – got the word out to the local militia there.

Daniel came to tell me the news. We are waiting to hear more.

"This is it," he said. "It must be."

21st April
It began in Lexington. The troops marched in and the patriot militia was waiting for them, outnumbered but standing up to them. Then they opened fire and eight

colonists were killed before the troops were ordered to re-assemble and move on to Concord.

By that time, the word had spread. The patriots were ready for them. I can only imagine what it must have been like, to be part of a patriot army that sent the British into defeat. Defeat! The troops have retreated here to Boston and are fortifying it to ensure that the 'rebels' outside can't get in.

It seems to be impossible to get out of here, too. I must find Daniel and discover what the best course of action is.

29th April

This will be the last I write in here for some time, I imagine. The government is issuing passes for travelling in and out of Boston, and many patriots are leaving, to join the forces gathered outside or simply to be away from the gathering of British forces here. Loyalist families from outside the town are flocking here for that very reason – to be safe.

I thought perhaps William might go, although they know he is a militiaman and would only allow him safe passage out of the city if he handed over his weapon first. But he and Martha are staying here – for now, anyway. She is going to have a baby, we heard, and his first duty is to be with her.

At first when I heard this I thought he was a coward, but I have been thinking about my father, and his leaving before Sarah was born, and I have to admit that William is not nearly as dreadful as he used to be.

Uncle Alexander and Aunt Charlotte are staying here too – they have the tavern, and they're not leaving that. And they will keep Sarah safe – Aunt Charlotte has promised me that.

When I told them I was leaving they were not surprised. I am not the only one going. I will join Daniel and some of the other boys – no, men – later.

"You're being brave," Sarah said. "Just like –" She caught herself. I knew what she meant. Just like our father, the dream version of him our mother wanted us to believe in.

I don't feel brave, but there is something else inside me. Something that tells me this is the right thing to do. I think of all the things that have happened over the past years, and all the things that will keep happening if they are not stopped. Liberty means putting an end to it. Liberty means being able to breathe. Liberty is worth fighting for. I can feel that as sure as I can feel my fingers and toes itching for action.

I am entrusting this book to Sarah and I hope that the next time I see these pages, America will be free.

Boston, 1783

My dear brother,
I had put this book away for safekeeping and then for years
I could hardly bear to look at it. It reminded me of you, I
suppose, although in retrospect that sounds so foolish. I
never needed a book to think of you. Even after you left,
there were echoes of you everywhere. I would think of
something I wanted to tell you, or something I wanted to
tease you about – and then realise with a shock that you
weren't there.

I have been thinking about you more and more these past
months for two reasons – the first is that I am about to have
a baby. I can almost see your face light up – I know you
never had much time for all that talk about marriage and

children, but you would have been happy for me, I know. I think you would be pleased to know I have married Daniel, if amused that my childish fancy proved to be fateful after all! I never dreamed it myself. I think perhaps you had something to do with it – when he returned, limping back to town a few years ago, after he could no longer fight, we spoke of you. We remembered you. I remember so clearly how it was when we were growing up, and how important it was that you and I could speak of Mother even when Uncle Alexander and Aunt Charlotte never mentioned her name. This was something similar, and we became friends first, and then when he asked me to marry him there was never any question that I might say anything other than yes.

The second reason I have been thinking of you is that the war is finally over – not officially, but there are talks and negotiations and it seems as though the end is finally in sight. And that we have won. It has been long and hard and dreadful. That first year, when we stayed in Boston, I knew so quickly it was a mistake. We were cold and starving, because it was so difficult for supplies to travel in and out; we were cut off from the world. It wasn't until March of '76 that George Washington and the Continental Army took back Boston, and the British left. And then we began the business of waiting out the war and doing what we could. I made so many blankets and uniforms for our men that my hands ached.

What a petty complaint that is, now that I see it written

down. You must understand that I hated them for such a long time. Oh, I understood what they were doing and why they were fighting. Liberty. Our natural rights. Our right as Americans to be separate from the great and powerful British Empire. I knew all that, but something had happened to my heart when the news came of what had happened near Bunker Hill. At the time – only June, not even two months after you had joined the patriot forces (I struggle to remember now, but I don't think they were even called the Continental Army then) – it was the greatest loss of manpower the British had seen, even though they won the battle, and that was what gave us hope. But of course many patriots died too, or were captured – I am grateful now that you weren't taken prisoner, because there are so many awful stories about prisoners I have heard over the last number of years. Dr Warren died – that was the one people talked about, of course, the great loss to the patriot cause.

As Daniel tells it, the patriot forces were retreating when you were hit. As he tells it, you were watching out for him – and if you hadn't been there, he would have died instead. Sometimes, he says, he wishes he had.

I don't know if this is true. I remember how Mother always told us about how brave and strong and handsome our father was, and how it was a lie that kept us warm at night, and I know you always wished I had never discovered the truth. I wonder if this is a story Daniel tells me to make your death have a purpose, in some way. I've never asked, and I don't think I ever will. I know he was your dearest friend – perhaps the only other person in the world you would have saved in that way except me. I think about when you were younger, when we were so young and before this awful war broke out, and when you took to wanting to be a doctor. I always thought it would be hard for you to save the people you hated, or didn't think were worthwhile – but I never once thought you wouldn't go to the ends of the earth to save the people you loved. So maybe it's true, or maybe it's a beautiful lie – maybe I don't ever need to know.

I know war is awful, not glorious. I have seen too many men return, hungry and bitter, too many families grieving, too many dreams shattered. It has been a long, long war, and our side have not always had enough food or shelter or gunpowder, and so often news would come of another British victory that seemed to spell the end. And then there would be an American victory, and there was hope again – but everything always came at such a high cost.

The year before last, in October, there was a battle in Yorktown in Virginia that decided it. The British commander, Lord Cornwallis, surrendered to Washington – they say he was so ashamed of being defeated that he sent his second-in-command to do the job for him. There was a temporary treaty signed last year, in Paris of all places, and the delegates are still negotiating a permanent agreement. The French have helped us through this war – without them, I'm sure, things would have been much worse.

I wish so much I could fold up this letter and slip it inside a pocket or into a book for you to find later. I wish I could have known you longer as a man and not a boy – you were only just becoming one when you left to fight, and now I am older I find myself wondering what you would have become. What you could have done.

I can't know what was in your heart that day. But this is what our government, our 'experiment in democracy' as they call it, said a year later when they wrote 'A Declaration by the Representatives of the United States of America, in General Congress Assembled':

"We hold these truths to be self-evident, that all men are created equal, that they are endowed by their creator with certain unalienable rights, that among these are life, liberty and the pursuit of happiness."

I think you were fighting for these things – the first two, anyway. I wish you'd had more time for the third, and I'm sure if you had been alive to read the Declaration, to hear it read out, you'd have been baffled by its inclusion. Perhaps we need liberty before pursuing happiness is a possibility. Perhaps.

This new fledgling nation of ours is fragile, but I hope for your sake it lasts.

I hope it is worth the price we have all paid.

Your loving sister, always,

Sarah

France

Paris, 1789

30th April

Madame Mournier was most delighted that it was my birthday today. She is always pleased whenever someone has a birthday, but most especially when it presents her with the opportunity to teach us a lesson. "Named, of course, for Saint Catherine of Siena," she said – just as she said this time last year! – and then went on to advise us all to fast and be virtuous and say our prayers, just as Saint Catherine would have.

Émilie, who is my best friend, was furious. None of us in the little school is terribly poor, but it is still all very well for Madame Mournier, who is plump and healthy, to lecture us on the need to dwell on our spiritual salvation instead of our earthly bodies. The price of bread – the cost of everything, it seems! – is rising and rising. Maman is worried, even though Papa continues to reassure her that all will be well. He has tried explaining to us exactly how the elections work but it seems very complicated and gives us both a headache. He is hopeful of becoming one of the deputies.

Émilie dared me to ask Madame Mournier to explain to us what was going on but I am not nearly brave enough to risk her wrath. I can imagine what she would say and it would not be kind. Madame is very firm on matters which are not suitable for young girls. What use would it be to a girl to know what happens when men gather to speak with the king? (I am not sure if we really want to know or if it would simply be preferable to listening to her compare us unfavourably to the saints. Émilie and I giggle too much, and the saints never seem to be laughing in any of the pictures.)

30th April (later)

Papa and Maman are having one of their very loud conversations about Monsieur Réveillon's factory. We saw – and heard – the protestors on Sunday on our way home from Mass and last night, it is said, they attacked his home and he had to flee.

"What else does he expect?" Papa said, and then there was something about workers' wages. "People are starving, Sophie, and he talks of paying them less!"

"Those men on the street didn't die of starvation, Georges!" Her voice gets shaky and high when she's upset.

"Things will improve." He has been saying this for months now.

"So you keep saying!"

"The Estates are meeting soon! And Louis will see what's been going on. He'll make things right." The king's name is Louis – Louis XVI.

Maman muttered something which I could barely hear but which sounded a lot like, "The troops that killed those men were under his command."

She must be right – the king has command of everything – but Papa seems sure that it is ministers or the queen, Marie Antoinette, who are to blame for anything that goes wrong. That if they can just explain to the king how unfair it is that the taxes fall on us and not on the richest people, things will be better. That if the king knew that people were suffering instead of just stirring up trouble, he would want to help them.

I don't know what to think. Madame Mournier would say these are not things for girls to think about. I should be thinking about how I can make myself useful to Maman. I should be saying my prayers or practising my Latin.

Instead I am sitting on my bed writing in my diary, trying very hard not to cry. Papa and Maman are too busy with what is happening outside our home to remember that today I am eleven.

3rd May
Today is always a sad day.

4th May
When I was little it was just me and Papa. In those years he was a physician, before he began writing his complicated essays about philosophical matters. When I was eight he met Maman, who at first I did not want to call Maman – every time I said the word, it was as though my mouth was full of bitter ash.

My real mother was called Marie Elisabeth – isn't that a pretty name? Papa met her when he first moved to Paris. When I was little he would tell stories about her. She had fair hair like the sun, and was a natural beauty – not like those ladies who drown themselves in jewels and weave complicated things into their wigs. He says I look like her, even though I do not think I am at all beautiful. Perhaps I will be when I am older.

Before I was born there was another baby, born dead. Papa blamed the midwife, and, perhaps, himself for not being there at the time. When I was born he was there watching over the midwife like a hawk, as he puts it.

I was healthy but my mother soon grew feverish. Papa thought he knew what was wrong with her but it was too late. She died three days after my birth.

Yesterday we said prayers for her and Papa seemed more agitated than he usually is on the day. I didn't say anything. My throat was already too closed up with sorrow. I never knew my mother but I do wish she was still alive – but then he wouldn't have married Maman and it is wicked to wish her gone, surely.

Perhaps Papa is anxious about the elections. They are still taking place in Paris, but Emile's uncle, who is a lawyer from Languedoc, is already on his way to Versailles for the meeting tomorrow. I wonder if the king himself will be there, ready to close the door firmly shut on any latecomers, the way Madame Mournier sometimes does?

8th May

Papa has come home full of talk of what needs to be fixed in Paris. It seems to be about knocking things down – that customs wall everyone resents, which is a wall around Paris, built to prevent smuggling, with tax collectors guarding the gates – and the Bastille prison looming over us all. He makes grand gestures with his arms, as though he is a giant ready to reduce a fortress to dust with one mighty blow.

I think he has been drinking.

12th May

Émilie's family knew one of the workers who died in that protest outside the factory. Today after school she told me that her family is thinking of leaving Paris.

"Forever?" I said.

"Perhaps." She was twisting her handkerchief in her hands. "They're worried."

"About what?"

She looked to the sky. "Everything."

When I arrived home Papa was reading one of his favourite pamphlets over and over again, saying the words out loud. It is all there on the first page, he says, the key to it all: "'What is the Third Estate? Everything.'"

Émilie's and his are different kinds of 'everything' but I think they are linked somehow.

The Third Estate is what Papa wants to be elected to. The other Estates are for nobles and clerics, important people. People who matter. This has always been the way of things. Now, though, it feels there is a wind sweeping across the city. Perhaps the whole of France. It wants things to change.

But the king has the whole of the army and rules by the grace of God. They say when he was first crowned he would touch the sick and heal them – which Papa scoffs at but Madame Mournier insists is true. But, if it is true, then how could anyone dare disagree with him on anything?

14th May

I hope Émilie does not leave. They are still considering it. This evening she had dinner here.

We passed by some beggars on the street and they couldn't have been that much older than us. Their arms were so thin and their clothes so ragged that they barely looked human. And then one of them – I couldn't even tell if it was a boy or a girl – looked at me and held my gaze for a moment before turning away. Something horrible churned in my stomach.

Things have been getting worse for everyone since the bad harvest, but this is the first time I have ever felt guilty.

We had less bread, and worse bread, and more expensive bread, at the table tonight than we might have had a year or two ago but we had some.

Émilie was very polite and thanked Maman and Papa for the meal. Afterwards we looked out the window at all the people going by, some in fine carriages, most shuffling along. A fight started between two men – we didn't catch quite how it started but one seemed to shout at the other and then their fists were all a flurry.

"Everyone is so angry," I said.

Émilie nodded. "At least they are still alive."

24th May

Papa is gone! It feels strange that it has finally happened. All of this has been going on for weeks, months really, ever since it was announced the Estates-General would be meeting, but now it suddenly feels *real.* He left for Versailles last night as a deputy and he is so pleased and excited, almost like a boy.

"Things are changing," he said to me and Maman before he left. "We've already won something. There are more of us than them."

After he left I was still thinking about what he'd said, and I asked Maman, "Isn't there the same number of them?" They are supposed to be equal: as many Third Estate deputies as the other two orders put together.

She shrugged me off. She has been not quite herself since he left. She retired to her bed earlier than usual, reminding me to extinguish the candle when I was finished reading, as she always does – as though I need reminding!

I was pretending to read a book about domestic duties – Madame Mournier would approve of the title – but instead I had found that pamphlet Papa was reading over and over. I don't understand all of it, but there are things in it he has spoken of. It says that the Third Estate – us, and almost everyone else, I suppose, we who are commoners, we who are not special – is like "a strong and robust man with one arm still in chains".

I dreamt about a man who looked like Papa but who was not him either. He was broad and strong, with a solemn face, thrashing about until his chains broke and he was free. I didn't dare tell Maman. She would tell me it was my own fault, for what I was reading.

27th May

Maman is still sad and distracted. She has not ventured outside of the house since Papa left.

What should I do?

3rd June

A letter from Papa! He says he is having trouble hearing the speeches people are making. Maman muttered that he should clean his ears.

I am not sure 'sad' is the right word for her these days. She stomps around the house and gets angry if I get in her way.

I know it is sinful to wish her gone but –

3rd June (later)

Good news from Émilie! They are staying in Paris. Her father has been spending more and more time in the Palais-Royal, where Papa used to go to talk to all others who were excited about the Estates-General, and he seems to have caught that sort of fever that they get. His face is full of hope. When he saw me he clapped me on the back, and spoke about Papa and the other deputies. "Things will get better," he said. "The king will start listening to them."

I am having all kinds of sinful thoughts and if anyone found out I would be punished immediately. Because, if the king is in charge because God says so, then he is in the right no matter what we say – unless the king is not really doing what God wants at all. Unless he is just a man.

12th June

Maman is going to have a baby.

She said it as though it was obvious and I should have already known. Somehow.

As though she has not been keeping secrets from me.

14th June

Sometimes I imagine running away.

I don't know where I would go.

In stories, people always run to Paris, not away from it.

22nd June

There have been more letters from Papa, so hastily scrawled that it is difficult to read them, but we have heard about it all in the newspapers anyway. The Third Estate have started calling themselves the National Assembly and have invited members of the other estates to join them. I can only imagine what would happen if we tried such a thing in Madame Mournier's schoolroom, knocking on the doors of mansions and even the palace at Versailles to ask the princesses and duchesses if they'd like to come and sit with us. They would laugh in our faces.

"This will end badly," Maman said after the first letter arrived.

And it looks as though it might. They were all locked out of the meeting houses and ended up in a tennis court, of all places – one of Papa's friends there, Dr Guillotin, knows the man in charge of it. They are going to keep meeting until – this is what the papers say, we had to check because Papa's handwriting was downright illegible on this point – "the constitution of the kingdom is established".

"What on earth does that mean?" Maman said irritably. "Georges is a fool."

She used not to think this. She used to nod and smile whenever he talked at length about how things should be. It is the baby that is doing this to her, I think. Now when I look at her I can see she is heavier. It shows in her face, too.

My mother died after I was born. Papa is a doctor, or was – he still carries all that learning around in his head – and he is not here for Maman now that there is a baby on the way.

What use is a constitution if this child dies? If Maman dies?

5th July

Émilie insists I am worrying too much. Today after Mass she persuaded Maman to let me go with her and her family to see the street musicians and the puppeteers, instead of straight home.

Her father is so glad they have stayed in Paris. "You

will remember this as a great time to have been alive," he told me and Émilie.

We twirled each other around in the streets and I could almost taste the possibility in the air.

11th July
It is all awful. I don't know what it is but it is awful. Noise and anger. The king has done something, and the people of Paris are angry.

13th July
My hands are shaking. I can hardly write. What has happened is that the king dismissed one of his ministers, a man whom everyone seems to like, and now they are gathering men from every part of the city and preparing to fight.

They are on our side, these men, but I worry what will happen when the king's forces crush them. I worry about what will happen to the deputies.

No. That is a lie. I worry about Papa. All I want is for my father to be here with us and not in Versailles having meetings and listening to speeches and making great plans for the country that cannot possibly come to anything.

17th July
The minister is back.

And the Bastille . . . It is like some strange dream. It

has always been there. Always. Looming over us like a dark cloud. It is now broken and battered.

The last few days have been awful and wonderful at the same time, which perhaps doesn't make any sense, but it is how they have been. Awful because of the anger and the rage and the madness in the streets, everyone looking for weapons, looking to fight. I wanted Papa to be here so badly. He might have fought, or at any rate might have known what to say to the men who wanted to know if we had anything that might be of use. (They were very kind when they saw Maman and realised she was with child, but it was still alarming.) There was talk of the clergy hoarding grain, which proved true, and then on Tuesday – the 14th – a crowd went to the Bastille, first to ask for weapons, they say, and then to take them, if necessary.

All this time the king's troops had done nothing, but they were standing guard at the prison ready to stop people.

This is not a quiet place, not like it is beyond the city walls and in the countryside where you could walk past fields instead of rows of houses. But that day was a loud one. There were cannons – which Maman insisted must belong to the royal troops but we later found out were ours, the *people's* – and a crash.

I have a confession to make, the kind that I dare not tell Maman or a priest. I know what the crash was. Maman was resting, and I crept outside, my heart pounding all the while. I can't explain exactly what took over me – I wanted to know exactly what was going on, so that I could tell Papa later. It seems silly now. There are already so many pictures of it, so many broadsheets fluttering around the place with descriptions of what happened. I didn't get very far. But I could see the crowds, see the Bastille, and just as a woman in an apron told me to go home where I'd be safe, I saw it. The great drawbridge came down, and everyone rushed at it, and then more noises, the sound of weapons being fired, and I froze for a moment before running.

I knew I shouldn't have been there. People were killed. (This I found out later. I did not see any of the bodies, and I was glad of it.) I trembled all the way home, and I slept fitfully. My dreams were strange, and I imagined the king – who looked a little like our priest – beckoning me towards him and saying: "Catherine, you have disobeyed me, and you shall be punished."

But then the next few days were full of – hope? Something large and exciting. And today the king himself came to Paris, looking not at all like the version in my dreams, and the new mayor of Paris gave him a cockade to pin to his hat – the red and blue of Paris on top of the royal white – and there were cheers and cannons. It was astonishing. It was still so loud, so full of energy, but so different this time. Not angry but triumphant.

There was a great chant of, "Long live the nation!" The nation.

Even Maman seemed happy.

21st July

Émilie's cousin has come to live with them. His father is the same uncle who is a deputy at the National Assembly and, even though he is a few years older than we are, he was impressed when I told him Papa was a deputy as well.

His name is Antoine and he is full of excitement about being in Paris. "This is where it is all happening," he said.

"What?" Émilie wanted to know.

"The Revolution," he said.

27th July

This morning Maman said, "I met Émilie's mother in the baker's today."

I was sewing, or trying to. I would much prefer to read or even practise my Latin verbs but I know I must learn how to sew properly and neatly. I didn't know if she expected an answer.

"She says her nephew is staying with them. Have you met him?"

I nodded.

She looked suspicious then, but said nothing. When I told Émilie about this, she said perhaps Maman is worried that he is a boy? We have shown him parts of Paris, the different churches and hospitals and prisons, and which shops are the best and which are better avoided, and I never thought to tell Maman that we were alone with him.

I don't know very many boys that aren't very small children. They go to different schools and sometimes the ones in the street are rude and shout things that would make you blush. Antoine is not like that. He is very clever and seems to know a lot about what is happening in France. He says in the countryside there are peasants attacking their noble landlords, that the deputies in Versailles are worried.

"Something will have to be done," he said, his eyes shining. He looked like Émilie's father, or Papa, when he said that.

I thought of the day outside the Hotel de Ville where everyone had cheered the king and the nation, and I thought I might understand what was in his eyes.

28th August

Oh, what a month it has been! The Revolution has happened.

There was the 4th of August. Between Papa's letters and all the newspapers we have heard so much about it but it is as though a wind has blown through the country and taken with it all of the things that made people angry. Except it is not a wind. It is the Assembly, and Papa is a part of it, and I am so proud I could burst. He wrote to us to say, "It is done. The feudal regime is at an end. Remember this day!"

There are no more special rights for the nobles or the clergy. We are all commoners now and equal. Equal under the law – except, I think, the king and his family, for he is still, after all, the king.

Then for a while all the deputies were working on a new piece of writing called 'The Declaration of the Rights of Man and of the Citizen', which has since been published in the papers. Antoine has taken to carrying around a copy with him at all times. I have just returned from dinner with Émilie's family and it was all we talked about. It is like the Bill of Rights they have in America, they say, and it is filled with lines about liberty and equality and the law. I don't pretend to understand it all but it is all so exciting. So full of hope.

28th August (later)

Maman has ruined it all. Just as I had finished writing in here, she asked why I looked so happy, and I told her.

She rubbed her swollen belly and said, "Catherine, you fool. Recite the first article for me."

"'Men are born and remain free and equal in rights'," I said. I could not recite the others if you were to ask, but that first one I could recall.

"Precisely."

"What do you mean?"

"*Men*, Catherine. This has nothing to do with us. None of this will make any bit of difference to us." She looked out the window, and when she turned back to me she had tears in her eyes.

I know she misses Papa. I know that the possibilities that have suddenly opened up for Antoine are not things I can have. But I would never have had them anyway, and I hate that she has taken this bit of joy and stamped on it until there is nothing left.

It feels as though everyone else is celebrating except us.

7th September

Émilie and I are in trouble again for whispering to one another and giggling. Madame Mournier is furious with us. She slapped each of us across the face but the sting has faded. I didn't care.

I know from how my skirts edge up my legs that I am growing taller, but that doesn't explain how much smaller she seems all of a sudden.

15th September

Maman grows bigger and bigger every day. I worry that the baby will come before Papa returns home. He visited us last week but then had to return to Versailles for important business. Everything is important business there, it seems.

20th October

Sometimes life feels so sluggish and then there are times when it all speeds up and everything is happening at once. This is how these past few months have been, but especially the past weeks.

The most important thing is that Papa is home. Perhaps the most important thing should be that the baby has arrived safely and Maman did not die like my mother, although we were worried for a day or two. But mostly it is so reassuring and safe to have Papa back. The Assembly has moved to Paris, because the king lives here now, instead of in Versailles. A lot of market women who were angry about the bread shortages marched all the way there, armed with weapons, and brought him back. They told the king they needed to feed their husbands and children, and demanded that he should help them. And he did.

Papa says when the women first arrived in Versailles he and the other deputies didn't know what to make of them, but it was clear they were exhausted and hungry. He sounds as though he understands why they might have been so angry and why some of them were so violent – there are some terrible stories told about what happened to the guards. It must be awful to be hungry and to know your children are too.

People are still saying awful things about the queen, how she is frivolous and careless and can't be trusted, but now she is in Paris too. The royal family and the women and the National Guard all marched back together, a huge crowd – well, the royal family were in their carriage of course. Antoine says it was extraordinary. I have asked him to describe it for me over and over, trying to imagine it, because that was the day Maman was in such pain and I had no idea what to do. They both feel like things that happened long ago, even though it has only been a fortnight.

I thought Maman would die. I really did. I ran for the midwife and I was sure that when we returned Maman would no longer be alive. She was, but the screams were awful – it was as though some wild animal had taken her over and was in unbearable pain. I remember screaming too, screaming for the midwife to make it stop, and she slapped me across the face.

Now everyone is so happy about baby Jacques, and they say he is handsome like Papa, and will grow big and strong like him too, so it is worth all the pain and trouble, I suppose. But how terrifying it is when it happens!

19th December
Papa and his friends from the Assembly have some of the strangest conversations. Today it was about

something one of them – I think perhaps his doctor friend – said about a new machine that could cut off people's heads in the twinkling of an eye.

Only a few days ago Antoine asked me if I had ever seen an execution. I think he was expecting me to say no and to squeal in horror, but I put my hands on my hips and said that of course I have, which is true. Hasn't everyone? Papa has always thought it indecent but there are always crowds at the hangings.

"Have you seen them beaten?" Antoine asked.

"Of course," I said again, even though I don't like to think about it. They break their bones first. The pain must be agonising. I know they are bad men who must be punished and that we must all learn from this, but it is awful.

"Have you ever seen a noble executed?" he asked.

I hadn't. They are beheaded instead, he told me. It is quicker. Maybe not as quick as the new invention might be, but it is different.

Despite all this talk of equality, though, it is a strange thing to try to make equal!

25th December
Christmas! Prayers of thanks to the king and to the nation.

Paris, 1790

30th April

I had almost forgotten about this journal until my birthday! It has been a busy few months. I have been helping Maman with Jacques. He cries a lot and I would much rather be spending time with Émilie or Antoine, but Maman insists. She says it is good practice for when I have children of my own. That seems very far away, which is just as well. I still remember how awful it was when Jacques was born.

Today I am twelve and Maman has bought a cake to celebrate the occasion. We are waiting for Papa to return home from the club. "You spend all your time there," she said to him last week, although this is not strictly true. But, when he is not at the Assembly, he does seem to spend quite a few of his evenings at the club, talking with many of the same people about France and the future. Antoine tells me there are several clubs in Paris now, all for men to sit about and talk about political and philosophical matters. I suggested that Émilie and I should start a club for young ladies to talk about such things, and he laughed. I got quite cross. I hate it when he treats me as though I am a child.

Oh! I think Papa has arrived home. Cake!

18th July

It feels like all of Paris is still in high spirits after the Festival of the Federation to celebrate one year since the Fall of the Bastille. There was a huge Mass and then speeches and music and dancing and eating. The king and queen were there and it was all quite exciting, although I grew tired after a while and it kept raining.

2nd September

Papa has decided Madame Mournier is no longer a suitable tutor for me, so from now on I am to be educated at home. I was afraid that she thought I was too troublesome but Papa thinks she is a "superstitious fool" (Maman told him not to say such things in front of me but it was too late).

For now Maman is teaching me, which mostly means she allows me to read Papa's books and some of the newspapers when I am not learning about how to take care of Jacques.

19th December

I adore Madame Aubry! She is my new tutor and she is nothing, nothing like Madame Mournier. She writes essays and plays and is teaching me how to do the same. She says there is no reason why a woman should not make her voice public, especially now that everything has changed and one no longer needs to be a noble in order to matter.

Émilie thinks she is eccentric but Antoine is impressed with her. She is less impressed with Antoine. She told me I must not think of marriage just yet, that I am far too young, which made me blush so fiercely I was sure my face would burst into flames. Marriage! To Antoine! Or at all!

But apart from such moments she is wonderful.

Is it terrible to wish she might be my mother?

I am writing her a poem for Christmas.

Paris, 1791

11th January

Antoine has been away for the last few weeks at home. I have missed him. I was trying to tell Émilie about one of Papa's books I read, which is about a man who wakes up in the year 2440 (can you imagine?) to find all the problems of Paris have been solved. Émilie looked a little bored. She wondered why I would read such a thing when I could read about people in love.

"In love?" I said.

"You must read this," she said, pressing a volume into my hands. "It will make you weep terribly." She said it as though it was a good thing. "Don't show it to your parents, though."

I recognised the name of the man on the cover – Rousseau – a writer Papa is very fond of. He died the year I was born. The year Maman died. In fact, I discovered that Papa has this very same book, all the volumes neatly lined up on his shelf, although high up, where he keeps his medical books and other things that I am not really supposed to read.

I started reading it secretly, because there was not much else to do, but I was glad when Antoine returned to Paris and we could talk about the other book. He has read it too – he reads an awful lot – and was glad to have someone to discuss it with.

I did not tell him about the book Émilie wishes me to read, which is called *Julie, or the New Heloise* and is about people in the Alps writing love letters to each other. It is full of passion and feeling and it embarrasses me to read it. I would much rather think about other things.

I wonder if he has read it.

6th February

It is Sunday and we are not in Mass. This is not the first time this has happened, but it is the first time that Maman and Papa haven't argued about it.

Madame Aubry has explained to me a little about how the clergy have been asked to take an oath to the new constitution. She says it is how they will adapt to live in this new nation, instead of clinging to the old ways. Most of the priests in Paris have taken the oath and those who haven't – they call them "refractory priests" – are not thought highly of. It is as though they are not loyal to the nation.

"But our priest took the oath," I said.

Madame Aubry shrugged. She is so elegant when she shrugs. "Perhaps the oath does not go far enough," she suggested.

There is a question I want to ask her tomorrow but I am almost afraid to.

9th February

I asked her. I asked, "Do you believe in God?"

She had a complicated answer which was to do with nature and reason. It sounded like the sort of thing Papa might say, or the sort of thing the characters in Rousseau's book might write. She didn't quite say no but she didn't say yes either.

2nd March

There was some kind of fight between some aristocrats and the leader of the National Guard, Lafayette. Antoine thinks there is a conspiracy to get the king out of Paris, to help him escape.

"Why would he want to escape?" I asked.

Antoine gave me one of those knowing looks that makes me feel like such a child. "Wouldn't you miss being in charge of everything?"

He is still in charge. He has to confirm orders and agree to things – he is still the king! But it is true – the Assembly is also making decisions. Making things happen.

Antoine reminded me that the queen is an Austrian. Her brother is the Holy Roman Emperor, who controls so much of Europe.

I let it sink in for a moment. I imagined if Jacques were grown up and in charge of a huge army. No one seems to believe the queen is loyal to us. But what if her brother is loyal to her and he doesn't like what is happening in France?

"Don't worry, Catherine," Antoine said, and then added, "Well – don't worry too much."

30th April

I feel so much older than thirteen. How strange.

26th June

Madame Aubry has suggested I write a play about the events of the past week. We have been to see plays together, sometimes about important moments like the Fall of the Bastille, and she says there will be plays about this too.

Antoine was right. The royal family have been plotting to escape. They are not on our side. Some people are blaming the queen still but Antoine thinks it is the king too. That he does not support anything the Assembly or the people of Paris are doing. It is hard to believe that he does, any more.

They disguised themselves and were trying to get to a fortress in the north of France, near the border, where they would gather forces and try to retake the country. That is what is being said. When they got to the town of Varennes, a postmaster recognised the king, and the whole family were brought back to Paris. The man's name is Drouet and Madame Aubry thinks I should write the play with him as the hero. He is a hero, really. Who knows what might have happened if he had not been there?

15th July

Both Papa and Antoine are furious about what has just happened. The Assembly has decided to "let the king off the hook" as Papa puts it.

The clubs have been circulating petitions saying that the king abdicated his post in June, that they will not recognise Louis as their rightful king. They are going to try to get more support.

There is a tight feeling in my chest that I think is about the injustice of it all. I have been playing with Jacques this afternoon and it helps a little. He smiles and is easily entertained. He doesn't know what's going on. I envy him.

18th July

It is too horrible for words.

Madame Aubry always says that the words help.

But I am not sure they do.

18th July (later)

Yesterday. It all happened yesterday. It feels like so long ago.

It was on the Champ de Mars, the same place we went to celebrate the anniversary of the Bastille falling. Maman stayed at home with Jacques but I wanted to be there with Papa and with the others I knew who were trying to speak up. It was just a petition. Just a protest. Just a way of saying that it is not just that the king is still king. He abandoned us. He can't be trusted.

Émilie's father was there, and Antoine. Antoine's father was not – he agrees with most of the Assembly, unlike Papa. I saw Madame Aubry too.

The National Guard were there too and they tried to get everyone to leave. For a while it was a little quieter, and then the crowd swelled. Papa knew some of the men leading the crowd – one of them is named Danton, that much I remember, a big loud man people pay attention to.

There were so many people there I could hardly breathe. Papa yelled at me to go home, for fear I might be crushed. Antoine took my hand and we tried pushing our way through the crowds.

And then the shots began.

And everyone was trying to get away.

They say that they were warning shots. That the National Guard – who are led by Lafayette, who is supposed to be on our side, who is a grand hero of the American Revolution – were just trying to "restore the peace".

My hands are trembling.

Papa escaped, with only a scrape or two. Madame Aubry was injured – some awful cuts and a broken arm.

Émilie's father is dead.

He is a good man.

Was.

Was.

20th July

I don't know what to say to Émilie. She keeps sobbing. This is not like the way she sobs over books – her entire body shakes and nothing anyone says can make it stop. And why should it?

3rd August

It is such a strange thing to know someone who died that day. There have always been deaths in Paris. I am not a child. I know that. People die for all sorts of things.

But I do not think Émilie's father or anyone there

that day did anything wrong. They say there were some people throwing stones at the guards. Maybe. All I remember is the sound of the shots being fired.

People have written about the day, printed pamphlets and newspapers about it, and they talk about everyone who died as though they were just any group of people and not individuals, each one of them.

9th October

That dreadful Lafayette has resigned as commander of the National Guard. Good. GOOD.

Papa is no longer a deputy. None of them are, any more. There is a new government, the Legislative Assembly. The old deputies are not allowed be part of it. They decided this for themselves. Antoine's father is staying in Paris, though. I think he is partly worried about Émilie's family and partly wants to be where decisions are being made. Where things are happening.

It feels like everything is breaking apart.

Maman tells me I must stop moping. She wants me to entertain Jacques while she makes dinner. He is two years old now, and cries less than he used to, but has taken to screeching when he doesn't get his way.

5th December

Antoine tells me the things Papa won't. About how there might be war. About the nobles who have fled the country who might return to try to change things back to the way they were.

Madame Aubry is pleased with my work but she is also distracted sometimes. I think she has become frightened since that terrible day. Her arm has healed but she still holds it strangely, and she is less inclined to speak honestly with me. I so wish I could go to those clubs that the men go to and listen to what they have to say.

Paris, 1792

19th January

There are riots over food again. Maman got caught up in one last week. People are saying all kinds of things about conspiracies. I don't know what to believe.

15th February

There is more talk of war. Austria and Prussia have allied themselves against us. It seems inevitable.

Antoine wants to join the army and fight. When he talks like this it all seems too real. If there is a war, if those other countries want to fight us, we will need more soldiers. And some of them will die.

I do not want Antoine to die. Or Papa. I don't want anyone to.

20th February

When I told Madame Aubry I was worried about Papa dying (she had asked what was troubling me – she said my face was pale and I was distracted, which must have been true as I hadn't heard anything she had said before this), she sighed and said that this is how men solve their problems. By fighting.

"They seem to talk a lot about it first," I said. I was thinking of the great speeches Papa makes, or the way those men like Danton talk to the crowds to spur them into action.

She laughed. I didn't think it was very funny.

30th April

It is my fourteenth birthday and we have been at war with Austria for more than a week now. I say 'we' as though I had any say in it. Papa does not think especially highly of the new government. "It was a mistake to step back," he said last night. "They could have benefitted from our experience."

"Whose idea was it?" I asked. It does seem odd, that they would all agree that the new government should have only new people in it.

He says it was a man named Robespierre. "He's too idealistic for his own good," he said, shaking his head.

"The deputies in there now . . ." He threw up his hands. "They won't last. We need a strong government to keep us safe. To protect everything we've created here."

"Do you think . . ." I was almost afraid to ask, but I had to. "Do you think they'll win the war?"

"Georges!" Maman said sharply. She appeared in the doorway, her arms folded. "It's late. Come to bed. Leave Catherine alone."

She worries that I will worry if he tells me things. I worry more when there are things I don't know.

20th June

My heart is pounding.

It has been the most exciting and terrifying day.

People have been furious with the king because he has been using his veto to stop so many of the things that the government wants to do. Why should he have this right, when it's clear what the people want?

I knew there was a plan for many workers to go to the Tuileries Palace, where the royal family live now, and plant a liberty tree, and to protest against the veto. Antoine had told me. Papa knew of it, but I think he is wary of some of the men involved. He much prefers the discussions around a table to the rowdiness of the crowd. And he would never have dreamed that Madame Aubry and I would have been out walking in the city today when the march to the palace began.

Some of them wore rags; others were dressed in simple clothing. Many of them carried pikes. There was even one man who went by with a calf's heart on his pike – someone later told me it was supposed to represent the heart of an aristocrat. A woman that Madame Aubry knows shouted out to us to join them and, as though we were pulled by invisible strings, we found ourselves as part of the crowd. Another woman pinned a tricolour ribbon to my dress.

We marched alongside the rest of them, and I thought of how Maman would wish me to be at home being good and quiet and well-mannered. With every step I grew more convinced this was better. I could hardly breathe at times; the stench of the city and all its people is always worse in the summer, and we were so crowded together, but it seemed like a small price to pay for what ran through my veins as I joined in the shouts: "Down with the veto! Long live the nation!"

When we arrived at the palace the tree was planted, and those at the front asked to be seen. The king eventually emerged, wearing a red cap of liberty. Others managed to get inside and to see the queen; she was dressed in fine clothing and surrounded by other fine ladies. I imagined that man with the heart on a pike and how he might wave it in their faces.

Perhaps it doesn't sound like much now that I write it down. Except that we have shown them today that we are not nothing. We are not meek and quiet and waiting for those in power to make decisions. We are loud. We are powerful.

For the first time I feel a part of something.

On the way home Madame Aubry and I couldn't stop talking about it. There was something in the air, some great hope of the things to come.

Then she stopped and looked at me. "Your dress is ruined, Catherine. Your mother will be furious."

It wasn't that dreadful once we looked at it. We went first to her home – she rents a room in an apartment above an old friend of Papa's – and mended the tears. There was dirt on my face I hadn't even realised was there. Maman was not impressed to see us home so late, but Madame Aubry reassured her we had lost track of time.

Now it is late – although Papa is still at the club – and I can't sleep. My arms and legs are still tingling with energy. It is like stepping into a different world, to have been part of what happened today.

Some of them have named themselves "sans-culottes", because they don't wear gentlemen's breeches. Instead they wear workers' trousers. Sans-culottes. Ordinary people who want things to be different and are prepared to fight for it.

12th July

Something is coming. Things cannot keep going as they are. We all know it.

It has been nearly three years since it all began. What a time to be alive!

2nd August

The foreign armies are getting closer to Paris. They have threatened to destroy us all if we do not submit to the king – the lying, traitorous king. He has been writing to the foreign armies for months – we all know it.

Papa has been meeting with others from this section of the city, and there is something being planned. He is distracted yet there is a light in his eyes that I haven't seen in a long time.

I asked Antoine what was going on when we were out walking yesterday. "It's none of your concern," he said, but kindly. "Please, Catherine. It's not the sort of the thing you need to worry about."

I didn't dare tell him I was there that day at the Tuileries. He was there, he told me afterwards. It was such a large crowd I wouldn't have spotted him, and he never would have thought to look for me. But I did say, "Why not? I'm not a child."

Sometimes I feel like I have been telling Antoine this for as long as I have known for him. For as long as we have been friends.

He surprised me then by saying, "No, of course you're not. But you are very precious. I don't want anything to happen to you."

What is going to happen that will mean something might happen to me? Why won't anyone tell me anything? Although I must admit I was too taken aback by how kind Antoine was being to ask those questions at the time.

9th August

It is late. The bells are ringing out. Something. Something is happening. I can feel it.

10th August

I am not a warrior woman, although I know there are some out there, looking like the kind of figure one only sees in books. I ran outside early this morning to see what was going on and Papa, among a group of men from our area, sent me back inside. "Stay with Maman and Jacques," he said.

"What's going on?" I asked.

"A revolution," he said.

I wanted to ask, 'Another one?', but he was already gone.

I slipped out again later that morning, hoping to join the crowds heading for the palace, but a group of boys scoffed at me. They had weapons. They know how to fight. What good would I be? There are women there who look like Joan of Arc, who wield pistols and swords and pikes, and I have only my fists.

I know they are right but it stings.

Madame Aubry has been telling me to write, write it all down and turn it into something, and that is how I will make a difference. Sometimes we read the different newspapers and journals together and it feels like a possibility. I can see how the words inspire people. How sometimes someone will put an argument down on a page and it will change the way you look at the world. In the years before the revolution happened, she says, there were books that changed how people thought. She has encouraged me to read some of them, though there are some she says are far too wicked for a young girl.

I know that words do make a difference. But they are not everything. And right now I wish I was outside with Papa. With Antoine too – I am sure he is among them. This is what has been whispered about and plotted. This is it.

10th August (later)

Papa arrived home covered in blood.

It was not his own.

I wanted to ask if he knew whose it was.

If he had killed someone.

I know people died. People supporting the king died today, in all kinds of ways. There were heads on pikes carried around the city, their eyes still open. Our neighbours were at the palace stripping the dead bodies of their clothes and taking whatever else they could find.

I don't know if any of them died because of Papa.

"What happened, Georges?" Maman's voice was shrill.

He poured himself a glass of something strong. He was still wearing his stained clothes as he sat down. "We won," he said.

"What does that mean, you won? What does that even mean?"

"The king has no more power," he said. "We have it. We. The people." He thumped his chest.

Maman took a deep breath. "The king has always had power. He always will."

Papa shook his head. And he looked so proud in that moment. "Things have changed."

25th August

There will be a new government. For now it seems as though everything is in the hands of the Commune, the local government of Paris. Papa knows many of the men there; some of them are men from the clubs.

Antoine knows a number of them too. He says they are imprisoning those who supported the king. The royal family are imprisoned too, put away in an old monastery called the Temple. "Even the children?" I asked. There are two – a boy and a girl. The princess is close to my age. Antoine explained that the son must be "dealt with" as well as the king. He is next in line for the throne and those who support France having a king want him to take over. But we don't want a king at all. Not any more.

"It seems like an awful way to think about people," I said.

"And how do you think they think about us?" he said.

I know the answer. They think we are nothing. If they think anything at all.

13th September

The traitors in the prisons have been tried and executed. Hundreds of them. Maybe even a thousand.

It sounds awful.

They were torn apart by a group of sans-culottes.

Antoine says it is necessary. The enemy was getting closer. We need to stamp out the enemy within France. We need to protect what we have.

But it all seems so rushed and sudden and I can't help but wonder what if some of the people in the prisons weren't guilty after all. How can it be possible to hold so many trials so quickly, and to find so many that deserve death?

28th September

We live in a republic now, a glorious republic. Papa has been elected to the Convention, the new government, along with many of the men from the Commune and the clubs.

I am trying to be happy about this. Papa is delighted, and Maman has come around somewhat. But what happened in the prisons has scared Émilie's family away. They are worried about what "the mob", as they put it, will do next. Antoine thinks they are fools. "It's only the enemies of the Republic that need to worry," he said. "They are scum. They should worry. We're patriots."

I don't know how much of this he told Émilie's mother. I know he had a fight with his father, because his father is leaving Paris too. They are all going, except for Antoine.

"I wish he'd come with us," Émilie said, red-eyed. "I'm going to worry so much about him. And you too."

I hugged her tightly. "You don't need to worry about us."

"I'll come back for your wedding," she said slyly.

"Émilie!" I pretended to be horrified but the truth is I know she is not the only one who has such thoughts.

I also know that Antoine's first love is France. And perhaps mine is too. Sometimes it is just exhilarating to think about what is happening here. We are setting an example for all of Europe – the whole world, even!

But it is frightening too. Perhaps such things always are.

Paris, 1793

5th January

When I write letters to Émilie I tell her things about Maman being with child again, or about Jacques's new favourite game, or about something amusing that Antoine has said. I write sometimes about Madame Aubry. I write about what people are wearing, and what is the most stylish way to show that you are a good republican in Paris nowadays.

I do not write about moments like tonight, when a group of men from the club have gathered in our home to continue on a discussion about what to do with the king. When they say things like, "It is too dangerous to keep Louis alive."

21st January

There is a square that used to be named after Louis XV, the grandfather of the present Louis – Louis XVI. It had a big statue of him on a horse, but it has been torn down. Now it is the 'Place de la Revolution' and there is a machine with a large blade, named after Papa's friend, Dr Guillotin. I don't think he meant it to ever be used; it was someone else who actually built it. But it is known as a guillotine now, and it is how criminals are punished.

The criminals have to climb up the steps to the scaffold, and their hair is cut to expose their neck. And then they are strapped onto a plank and their head is pushed through a frame and a few feet above there is a blade ready to fall. And when the executioner pulls at the handle, down comes the blade, sharp and swift, slicing off a head in an instant. In the twinkle of an eye.

The head falls into a basket and the executioner holds it up to the crowd, still dripping blood, still with an expression on its face.

The crowd was large today. Large and victorious. People threw their hats up into the air and cheered when the head was held up. People ran towards the blood to dip their fingers and handkerchiefs in.

Today they executed the king.

I wept, though I am not sure why. I wept but I also cheered.

I understood why it needed to be done. And it is so quick. So quick.

26th February
Antoine is talking of enlisting in the army. We have added England to our enemies and the Convention has called for many more men to join and defend the country. And there are yet more riots over food, and we are hungrier than usual. I cannot sleep with the worry of it all.

I am not writing to Émilie about any of this. I am merely hoping it will all be over soon. We will win the war, and there will be enough food for everyone, and the Republic will be at peace. It feels close enough to taste.

28th February
He must be too young. He is not eighteen for another year. They couldn't possibly let him join.

I need him here. In Paris. With me.

14th April
Papa is so often tired these days. He looks as though he has aged five years since the Republic began. They are setting up groups to make things happen. The Revolutionary Tribunal. The Committee of Public Safety. They are trying to keep order and to keep the sans-culottes happy.

Antoine is still here. For now. He follows all the news about the war. He reads the papers and he talks to men who are in the know. But when I finally asked him to stay, he said he would.

I don't know if he is only staying because he thinks that perhaps someday we will marry. I am too young. We are both too young.

Even as I write it, I know I feel much older. History has sped up. We have lived through great and terrible things and we have aged more than we should have, seen more than we should have.

3rd May

I wonder what my mother would say, if she were alive today.

This year seems less sad than usual. I don't know why. I feel almost guilty. Perhaps it is that I have seen more death than ever before. Perhaps it is that I am happy more often than not when Antoine is around.

Maman, however, knew nothing of this and she decided I would keep busy by playing cards with Jacques. There are new cards now, new revolutionary cards, because we cannot have kings or queens any more. Instead of kings there are now 'Spirit' cards; instead of queens there are 'Liberty' cards; the knights have been replaced with 'Equality' cards of different kinds – Equality of Duties, Equality of Rights. I think part of why Maman wished for us to play was so

Jacques could learn all about republican virtues. It did occupy my mind for at least some of the day.

11th June

Papa seems happier now than he has been recently. There has been a struggle for power in the Convention and it seems his side – the Jacobins, after the club – have been victorious.

"We must root out the enemies of the Republic," he said.

It seems strange that there would be enemies even within the Convention, now that there is no king to defend.

17th July

We went to watch the execution of a young woman who murdered a journalist who has for many years been writing all sorts of things in his paper. His name was Marat. Papa knew him – he was one of them, a Jacobin. I think I saw him once or twice. He was stabbed in the bath. He let this woman into his house, imagining, I suppose, that she could do him no harm, and then she stabbed him.

After her head fell into the basket a man lifted it up and slapped it on the cheek. I couldn't help but gasp.

2nd August

Early yesterday morning Maman began screaming. It

had begun. I remembered when Jacques was born, and how she had survived that, even though it was awful. The midwife came and I ran to fetch Papa, but by the time we arrived home the baby was dead. A tiny blue creature that hardly looks like a baby at all.

"It came too soon," the midwife said, wringing her hands. "I called for a priest to baptise the child, but he . . ."

Papa didn't even let her finish. He laughed – a horrible cruel laugh. "What good would a priest do?"

She had no idea what to say to him.

The baby has already been buried. No prayers. Just a solemn declaration that we are sad not to have given the Republic a new citizen today.

25th August

All the unmarried men between the ages of eighteen and twenty-five are to go and fight. I am grateful Antoine is too young. The rest of us are to do what we can for the war, the Convention says. Papa has arranged for me to help sew tents for the soldiers. He calls it "doing your civic duty", which I am quite happy and proud to do, but I wish I could do something other than sew.

It means I am to see far less of Madame Aubry, which saddens me, but she has encouraged me to keep writing and reassures me she will see me soon.

2nd September

There is talk of other armies being formed, citizen armies, to safeguard the revolution. To attack its enemies, and to ensure food prices are controlled.

It feels sometimes as though people outside of Paris don't understand. There are uprisings in the countryside, superstitious peasants who want a king for France instead of a real government that actually listens to the people and actually represents us. And then there are the foreign armies, and all the counter-revolutionaries within France – sneaking around and trying to sabotage things.

I asked Papa today, "When will the revolution be over?"

He rubbed his chin and said, "I wish I knew. There's still a lot of work to do. We're creating a new order, a new France. And there are those in the Convention who think it is not happening quickly enough."

"And there are people fighting against it," I said.

"Exactly. We need to deal with the enemies of the revolution."

"How do you –" I began, and then stopped. Of course I knew what he meant. There is only one real way to deal with traitors.

18th September

The Convention has taken action. They have approved revolutionary armies of sans-culottes to be set up, and they have created a new law which means it is easier to arrest those they suspect of being "enemies of liberty".

"The people have spoken," Antoine said. He was one of the citizens who went to the Convention to petition them to do this. He spends a lot of time in the Jacobin club. Like Papa he is impressed with the president of the Convention, Robespierre. They call him The Incorruptible.

1 Brumaire (22nd October)
I told Antoine I was never going to get used to the new republican calendar, but he seemed concerned that this meant I was clinging to the old ways, so I am going to use both dates in here, old and new, to help keep things straight in my head. This is one of the Convention's latest decrees – we count time not from the birth of Jesus but from the birth of our republic, 22nd September 1792 (which we now call Year I). This is Year II. The months have new names, all to do with nature – Brumaire for fog, which we often have this time of year. Next month is Frimaire, for frost.

The names do seem fitting. They suit Reason, which we are supposed to celebrate now instead of the old superstitious ways.

24 Brumaire (14th November)
Something awful has happened.

I have not seen Madame Aubry since the new laws passed. A few days ago I went to her home and was told she had been arrested. Her neighbour said she was suspected of being a royalist.

"What proof did they have?" I asked. I could hardly believe it. She marched on the Tuileries that great day in June of last year – she didn't want a king for France at all!

When I told Papa he looked sad but said he had heard that she'd been arrested.

"Where is she?" I wanted to know.

"In prison, of course."

"But she supports the revolution! She always has!"

Papa looked at me solemnly. "Catherine. She must have done something to make suspicion fall on her." He sighed. "These are difficult times. Some people think the revolution has gone too far."

"Maybe it has," I said.

He slapped me across the face, and then pulled me towards him, tilting my face up. "Don't let anyone hear you say that."

8 Frimaire (28th November)
Over the last few weeks I have watched the enemies of the revolution go to the guillotine. They are sometimes aristocrats, and sometimes poor. Sometimes men and sometimes women. Some of them weep. Some of them pray, or raise their voices to address the crowd, make

one final statement before their head comes off.

I have seen it happen once where the blade had not been properly sharpened and the head did not come off entirely on the first attempt. It was horrible.

They executed the queen more than a month ago. She looked like an old woman. Like an ordinary old woman. At her trial there were terrible things said about her. They couldn't possibly be true. But maybe they were. I don't know any more.

Today I watched Madame Aubry climb those steps, her hair cut short, and I wanted desperately to be mistaken. Let it be someone else, anyone else, I prayed – although who or what I was praying to I'm not sure. God? Reason? The Republic?

I have heard the blade fall often, but it has never left me trembling.

I am trembling for her, because I do believe she meant well, even if she did say or do something that was against the Republic. But I am also trembling for myself, her former student, who might come under suspicion. It is important that I am a good citizen. That I show myself to be a good citizen.

Paris, 1794

22nd Nivôse (11th January)

There are voices – Papa has company. They are
discussing a newspaper called *The Old Cordelier*. I have
read it. Papa pretends not to have, but I know he has.
It is hidden. It says that things have gone too far.

"He's a silly child," Papa has just said. "The Terror
will continue."

Someone else says, "It must continue. How else are
we to rid France of the traitors?"

Antoine would agree.

I am not sure Papa believes what he is saying.

They are arresting so many people. It is difficult to
believe they are all enemies of the Republic.

And if they are, then is it a republic worth having?

4 Germinal (24th March)

There are those who think the revolution has gone too far and those who think it has not gone far enough. There were men executed today who fall into the second group, men arguing that more should be done, and it begins to remind me of schoolchildren who will only play with those who agree with absolutely everything they say, only it is far worse.

When Antoine talks about Robespierre, the man who seems to control whatever the Committee of Public Safety do, he speaks of him in glowing terms.

Papa has stopped speaking of him at all.

He has met with –

No. There are things it is not safe to write down.

My father is a good citizen.

21 Germinal (10th April)

It has taken me several days to gather myself.

I don't even know where to begin.

I am safe. At least for now. I am safe because I asked Antoine to keep me safe and he wants to marry me.

I would rather die than marry him.

No. That is a lie. A shameful lie. I might die if I do not. I might die if I dare open my mouth and argue with him about what he has done. I might die if he suspects I am an enemy of Liberty, of the Republic, of this Glorious Revolution. That is where his loyalty lies. Not to me. Not to my father.

Papa was a good man.

22 Germinal (11th April)

I had to stop writing yesterday because I was sobbing so hard I could hardly see the page and my hands were shaking. It seems impossible.

They are dead. That man who used to lead the crowd, Danton – that hero of the people! He is dead. The man who wrote in his newspaper about how clemency rather than brutality should be shown. And the men that supported them, the men that were seen as a dangerous threat to the Republic. They are dead too. Each in the twinkle of an eye.

Papa was one of them.

I will never forgive myself for even hinting to Antoine that Papa was starting to doubt the Republic. I thought I was being so careful. But I fear he had something to do with it, that he provided evidence to the tribunal against Papa.

I dare not ask. He speaks of Papa in such awful terms, as though the two had never met, as though they had not spent much of the time agreeing with one another.

I miss him. I miss him so much.

22 Prairial (10th June)

There are new laws. Who needs evidence when you

have suspicion? Who needs justice when you have your precious revolutionary virtue that will no brook no opposition?

It is dangerous to write this. I know. I know.

27 Prairial (15th June)

Sometimes it seems as though there is so much blood on the streets of Paris that we will drown in it. This city will never be clean. There will forever be a stain upon it.

Antoine cheers. It energises him, all of this.

I hate him. How will I ever bear being his wife?

1 Thermidor (19th July)

I cannot take it any more. I cannot take Antoine supporting this man who so many people fear. The man who controls the Committee of Public Safety – ha! What a name for what it really is. It does not keep us safe. It keeps them safe.

9 Thermidor (27th July)

A number of men came to the house looking for Antoine just now. Maman and Jacques are out, visiting a friend of hers. She prefers to be in other homes these days, places where Papa's absence is less noticeable.

I told them Antoine was not here, that he does not live here. "We are not yet married," I said, my voice shaking.

"He is one of Robespierre's associates, yes?" one of them asked.

"Yes."

"Fiercely loyal to him?"

"Yes. Fiercely." I almost spat out the word.

"And what about you, mademoiselle?"

I was sure there was a right answer. I was sure they wanted me to profess my loyalty to that wretched Robespierre, to the Committee, to the Convention. I know what happens to those who don't.

I imagined Maman and Jacques returning home and finding me gone. I imagined Antoine discovering I was not the docile creature I have been pretending to be ever since Papa's death. And I didn't care.

"If there is one neck that deserves to see that blade, it is his," I said. I braced myself for them to take me away. It was a foolish thing to say.

They laughed. I couldn't believe it. I was sure this was the prelude to something much worse, something more sinister. Instead they turned around and left.

I don't know if there is anything left for me to hope for. It feels like one of those moments where everything will change, but there have been so many over the last five years that I have lost track. And what does it matter, really, if we have no king when we have a dictator instead? What does it matter if we are free but we cannot say what we think for fear of being turned over to the executioner? What does it matter if we are all equal in death?

What does it matter if the people we love are gone?

10 Thermidor (28th July)

They arrested him. The Convention have turned against Robespierre and his followers in the Committee of Public Safety. At last.

I thought it would make me happy, to watch. I thought perhaps the heaviness in my heart would lift. That awful Robespierre's jaw was bandaged up – they say he had tried to kill himself when he was arrested – and before the blade fell the executioner tore away the bandage and he roared like an animal. And then there was nothing.

They have arrested others. I know they will take Antoine too.

15 Thermidor (2nd August)

It is over. The Terror is at an end. That is what they say, anyway. They have rid the city of Robespierre's devoted followers. There must have been a hundred of them brought to justice.

Justice. That is not the right word for it at all.

Antoine was one of them. I couldn't look. There has been too much blood. Far too much. We are still at war and I wish I could believe that things will get better but I trust no one nowadays.

I have been thinking about the carts they brought

the prisoners to the guillotine in. I have been thinking about the wheels, turning over and over on the ground, the same things happening over and over.

This wheel has turned too often. Far too often.

I don't know if we are back where we started, or further down some road that may eventually lead to peace.

I want to believe it was not all in vain.

But I trust no one and nothing nowadays.

Ireland

Wexford, 1798

2nd February

I have a question for you, blank page, and it is this – have you ever wished to know a secret, and then, having uncovered it, regretted wanting to ever know it?

I know there have always been things my father and brothers know that they don't tell me. I am – as Tom insists on reminding me whenever he gets a chance – the runt of the litter. The youngest – not yet fifteen – and I have always been small for my age. Tom is sixteen and John is eighteen – both big and strong and fond of fighting. I would be too if I had their strength.

My mother has a whole range of names for me – her "precious boy", which makes me sound like a piece of jewellery, or when we're speaking Irish it's "a mhuirnín" or "a stór" – my darling, my precious – which makes me sound like a baby cradled in her lap. She has told me of how she was worried I would die when I was a baby so many times that it has started to lose all meaning. It feels like a story instead of my life. That happens sometimes when things are said over and over. You forget what parts are true and what parts have been added on as time goes by.

A few years ago something happened around here. There were men who were part of a secret organisation who marched into the town to free two prisoners, and the army opened fire and lots of them died – some on the spot, some later, from their wounds. I didn't see it happen but I have heard so much about it that I feel like I was there. The corporation put up a monument to a man called Major Vallotton, who died defending the town from the rebels. John says they only put it up to prove that they were loyal to the Crown and that it's all nonsense. It makes the Major sound like a hero who was just doing his job when really he lost his temper while he was supposed to be parleying with John Moore, the man representing the rebels. He struck him with his sword and then Moore wounded him with a scythe – both men died a few days later. But the story has been told over and over again and, as with all stories, how much is real and how much is made up?

What I do know is that secret organisations sound exciting and daring but also are more trouble than they are worth. Especially now.

3rd February

"Robert, a stór," Tom said to me this morning, mocking the way Mother says it, "have you finished quivering in your boots?"

I was not "quivering in my boots" yesterday when he and John told me. It was just a shock. Perhaps it shouldn't have been. I know they have been stealing away after dark to the secret gatherings that people whisper about but don't dare speak of aloud.

All right. I suppose I was a little frightened, but I will only confess that here, and never aloud. But why shouldn't I be? We have heard the stories of what has happened in Ulster, how many people suspected of plotting rebellion were beaten or killed, how many men were locked up and charged with sedition. The United Irishmen are an illegal organisation and has been for years. To be found to have sworn the oath is a dangerous thing.

There. When I write it down like that it seems clear that it is no foolish thing to be afraid of joining them. If only I was as capable of expressing myself so well in person!

When Tom said that, though, I stared at him and

then retorted, "Are you calling me a coward?"

He laughed.

"I'm not," I said. Perhaps I am. But the last thing I wanted was for Tom to think of me as one. For anyone to think of me as one. I am almost a man, after all.

"So you'll prove yourself, then." By this he means I will swear the oath.

I should have said no. I should have said I didn't need to prove myself. Only I know I do.

"Of course," I said, as though there was no doubt whatsoever in my mind.

5th February

I have not yet been initiated, but I know it is only a matter of time. There was a meeting last night and I pretended to be ill. I am not sure whether they believed me or not, but I was so often ill as a child that they are used to it. John clapped me on the shoulder and told me to be better for the next time.

Tom told me today of how the Orangemen break into our churches and swear to murder us all. I don't know if I can believe him or not. I do know there are Protestants in the area who are bitter about the freedoms Catholics have been granted in the last few years, things it is strange to imagine not having now – the right to vote or bear arms. There are names that one hears – Ely, Ogle, Boyd – that make men like my father angry.

When I think about it, it should not be a great surprise that he and my brothers are members of the United Irishmen. They have always spoken highly of men like Wolfe Tone, the great republican thinker, even though he left the country years ago. He was one of the founders of the United Irishmen, back in '91. And one of my earliest memories is my father praising America for what they have done there, becoming independent from Britain, becoming free. And both he and my brothers speak eagerly of how the French have done the same and created a republic. I know about "republics" from studying the ancient Greeks and Romans, but that was a long time ago, and far away.

It all seemed like talk. That is the thing. It seemed like debate and discussion, but not something that we would ever do anything about. I always knew there were conversations they had when I wasn't around, but it never worried me too much. I was curious, but I never dared ask, because I am used to being on the outside. But lately the conversations had been growing more frequent, more hushed, and it seemed that if ever there was a time to ask, it was now. And as it turns out, asking my brothers (my father was still at work) what they were discussing is all it took for them to let me in on their secret.

This is not just harmless talk. This is saying directly that it is not right for us to be ruled by Englishmen and the servants of Englishmen. This is saying that we need a national government, that everyone in Ireland should have a say and that it shouldn't just be the Protestants who are allowed in the parliament. The association may be secret now, but what it wants – and what it is prepared to fight for – is not. We used to sometimes get copies of the *Northern Star* from Belfast, before it was closed down, and there is a Dublin newspaper called *The Irish Press* that I have seen at least one edition of in the house. We have a copy of *The Rights of Man*, which I have read parts of – perhaps I should read the entire thing now. Mr Paine has more experience of life than my brothers, after all.

7th February

Mr Paine says we live in "an age of revolutions, in which everything may be looked for". Somehow when I read his words it all seems so reasonable and clear. The current government is an unfair one. Just because things are this way right now doesn't mean they must stay that way. We live in a time where men can make their own destiny.

Then I think of all the men being put in the gaols, and the stories about what they do to suspected rebels. In some ways it makes me more determined to join my brothers, but in other ways it frightens me.

I do not want to be a coward.

12th February

I also do not want to die, or to be imprisoned and tortured. Does that make me a coward?

Every time Mother calls me "a mhuirnín" I can see Tom smirk, even more than usual. He has always been like this, ever since I was small and wanted to play with him and John. Sometimes they played at being soldiers, other times they organised games of hurling with some of the local lads. I was too frail, too much of a baby. Tom always said so.

"Never mind him," Mother used to say. "You'll be great friends when you're older." But we are older now and things are much as they always have been. Only now there is a chance to change all that.

20th February

I heard them talking about me late last night – my father and brothers. I suppose they thought I was asleep. I crept downstairs when I heard the voices, and that curiosity took over again. I was hovering outside the heavy door to the kitchen when I heard my name mentioned, and then I knew I had to stay and listen to what they were saying.

John had said something like, "We need all the men we can get", and then Father replied with, "Robert's just a boy. And not the bravest one, at that."

I heard a snort of some kind. I feel sure this was Tom.

John said, "He hasn't been given the chance to be brave."

"Your mother will never forgive me if anything happens to him."

There was a silence for a moment, and I couldn't bear it. I needed to know what kind of looks they were giving each other. So I pushed open the door. John and my father were sitting at the table, and Tom was pacing.

John spoke first. "Well, stop skulking in the shadows and come in."

I froze for a moment, but then, as if by their own accord, my feet crossed the threshold. And within minutes it was decided. I will join.

5th March

I have done it! I went to last night's meeting at a nearby inn with my father and brothers and it was astonishing how many familiar faces I saw there. Father is a grain merchant and knows many of the men in the town, but I had no idea how many of them were United Irishmen. Some of them we know from church and others are Protestants, but not the sort that agree with how things are run at the moment. We all swear to promote a brotherhood of affection "among Irishmen of every religious persuasion" – that is part of the oath I had to take last night along with other new members. It was the very first thing we did at the meeting, but I was glad, because otherwise I would have been nervous throughout, waiting for it to happen. Everyone there stood and took their hats off. I could feel their eyes on me.

After that we heard the minutes of the last meeting and reports from the Dublin society, and then we made plans to obtain more arms, especially for new recruits. John said to me, "There's a pike with your name on it."

It is strangely thoughtful for someone who has only recently decided I am worthy of knowing things about his life. It was only last week he told me he thought he would marry Jenny, who is the daughter of one of our neighbours, a merchant whose nephew was at the meeting last night.

"Marry her?" I said in surprise.

I knew they were friends. I am not that ignorant of what goes on. But the thought of John considering marriage seemed strange – especially to a Protestant girl. And I know our mother speaks of another girl – the butcher's daughter, who is a good Catholic (which is, as John notes, all we know about her; she barely ever says a word to anyone) – with a tone that suggests they will eventually be wed. John says once we have a republic and there is equality in Ireland, he will marry Jenny and no one will say a word about it.

15th March
I was woken this morning by Tom grabbing my throat

and demanding to know if I had told anyone anything. I was so shocked – and still half-asleep – that I could barely speak.

Thank God for John, who heard the shouting and intervened. "Let him go," he insisted, and then said, "For God's sake, who would he tell?"

I was slightly insulted but it is true. I have never had friends the way Tom and John have; it all comes from being so often ill. I have acquaintances – there are people I know through our father's business, where I help with the bookkeeping, or people who are Mother's friends and still think of me as a child. None of these are friends, though, and there is no one I have to share important secrets with. To be fair, I have never had important secrets until now.

It was John who took it upon himself to explain to me why everyone is so worried about spies and informers infiltrating the organisation now. A few days ago, in Dublin, there was a raid on a leader's house and the authorities in Dublin Castle seized many men, including delegates from other counties in Leinster. Our Wexford men were late to arrive, and for that they are tremendously grateful – they avoided capture and arrest. "And," John said, "it meant they couldn't give any of us up, either."

I like to think that our men wouldn't have given us up even if they had been captured but then I thought about pitch-capping and half-hanging and all the other things they could do to you. If you are suspected of treason then they will torture you until you tell them whatever you know. If I am truly honest with myself, I would probably confess anything I could think of just to make it stop.

It is strange how they call it treason. I have decided that it is the wrong name for it. It is the opposite of treason, really, what we are trying to do.

24th March

It seems it is clear there will have to be a rising of some kind, even though some of the leaders have been arrested. Lord Edward Fitzgerald, who shares his name with one of our local leaders, is in hiding in Dublin, they say. Wolfe Tone is in France in talks with the Directory there, their government, to seek their aid. They will help us, John says, because they support revolution against tyranny wherever it may occur, but also because they are at war with Britain and this would be a strike against them.

Whatever the reason, the idea of French aid is a hopeful one.

9th April

It is strange walking around the town and sometimes seeing faces of men that you know share in your secret. Mr Harvey, who is the landlord out at Bargy Castle, was in the town a few days ago and our eyes met. I imagine he does not know who I am, but I know he is one of us.

We wait to hear from Dublin what to do. If there is an uprising, and there must be, it will begin there. The government have declared the whole country under martial law and they are sending out troops to some of the more troublesome areas – not here yet, but it must only be a matter of time.

2nd May

We had to travel to Gorey these past few days to attend a funeral. Mother's uncle passed away – he had been ill a long time, so there was no great surprise or sorrow there. At the funeral people spoke about what has been happening there and elsewhere in the country. Someone who had come from Kildare had seen their neighbour pitch-capped the day before for being a suspected United Irishmen – or "croppy" as this man called it, because of the rebels' hairstyle. The republicans in France wear their hair cropped short too.

I keep picturing it. Pitch-capping involves hot tar being poured on your head – it is torture of the worst kind. It can get into your eyes too – the pain must be horrendous. Still, it's not as bad as what happens when the tar cools and then they pull it off you – along with all your hair and parts of your scalp.

This man was describing this to tell us how

dangerous things were for anyone who might be suspected of conspiring against the Crown, but John interrupted him and said, "If this is how they treat people, they'll cause a rebellion, not prevent one."

"Hold your tongue," the man said, leaning in a little closer.

I agree that it was a foolish thing for John to say out loud in a public place where anyone might have heard. But I agree with what he said. It all sounds awful but none of this is making me any less convinced that I have done the right thing.

There are others who have listened to what many of the priests are saying and handed over their pikes and sworn their loyalty to the Crown. I cannot do that.

"It was just an observation," I said in John's defence.

Tom was ready to launch into a tirade at that moment, I knew it, but it wouldn't have been wise. The man left us alone after that. I don't think he is an informer, but he is not one of us. The three of us stood together, brothers, by blood and by oath. I have stood between my brothers before, but never like that. Never as their equal.

6th May
Today at Mass the priest implored us all once again to hand over our weapons, if we were engaging in any sinful activities.

Afterwards, over dinner, Mother looked around the table and said, "I hope you were all paying attention earlier."

Father stared at her and said, "What do you mean by that?"

"What do you think I mean! They've sent in the North Cork militia . . . they're looking for any excuse to go after Catholics."

"There's Catholics in the militia too," John spoke up. "And the yeomanry." He didn't add that some of them have defected in the last few weeks – we know a few.

"Under the thumbs of their Protestant landlords, no doubt." Mother sniffed. "They wouldn't hesitate to hang you if they got half a chance."

"They've no reason to do anything to us," John said.

"What do you take me for?" Mother was furious. "I know well the lot of you have taken the United oath." She looked straight at me then, and I felt rotten. "Not the oath anyone should be taking these days." She means we should be swearing our loyalty to the Crown – not to a secret republican brotherhood determined to free the nation from that Crown.

"Don't concern yourself with it," Father said, which of course was exactly the wrong thing to say.

"Don't concern myself – when half the houses in the county are being searched and set alight? Don't concern myself?" She looked ready to hit him.

"That's exactly why we need to fight back!" Tom said, slamming his fist down on the table.

"Fight back? Fight back?" She looked around at all of us. "That's exactly why you need to keep your heads down. It'll be over soon."

"And then things can go on exactly as they always were," I said.

"Exactly," she said. "At least one of you has some sense."

"That's not what I mean," I said, but already Tom was talking over me, and then we were all speaking at once until finally Mother stood up and said, "To hell with the lot of you!" before leaving the house. She came home well before dark, but hasn't spoken to any of us since. The house is oddly silent.

7th May

She didn't say a word when we all left last night for the meeting. There is no news from Dublin yet about a date and some of the men are anxious. Even as there are newcomers joining us there are others slipping away, frightened by the troops and the searches and the tension that hangs heavy in the air. Something has to happen, and soon.

I decided I would try explaining this to Mother, but when I started to this afternoon, she cut me off. "Robert, there's no need for you to get caught up in this. You're just a boy."

149

I wish she would see me as I truly am – fifteen soon, no longer her dear sweet invalid son who needs all of her love and attention but gets no respect from his brothers. That boy no longer exists. That boy perhaps would have accepted things as they are, instead of realising that we live in a world where change is possible.

"Some of those lads in the Irishmen started off as Defenders," she went on.

John had told me about them – a Catholic secret society, and a bit rough sometimes.

"They're not interested in any of your French ideas," she went on. "They just want the Protestants out. People around here can hold a grudge forever."

She's right about that. Some people do still talk of the land that was stolen from their forefathers and given to the English settlers, but doesn't she see that this is all part of the same problem? That if we all unite we can bring about a better society, a better world, a nation that looks to the future instead of the past!

"That's not what we want," I said. And then I told her something I perhaps shouldn't have – about John's plans to marry Jenny.

"I thought you were the dreamer of the family," she said. "Her father will never agree to that. He might have argued for Catholics having the vote but he won't have his daughter marrying one of us, mark my words."

I think she's wrong. I wish I hadn't said anything. I told John, afraid he would hit me for it, and he just sighed. We agreed that she doesn't understand. She will. Soon.

21st May
There is news that soon in Dublin it will begin. We should know more shortly.

I am shaking a little bit as I write this. It is not in a cowardly way. It is exciting to know that it is almost time for all of this talk to come to something.

27th May
This is what we know: Perry has been arrested in Gorey, and Harvey, Fitzgerald, and Colclough here – all leaders who might give up names. But the king's troops are marching out of the town – there is something going on elsewhere, some disturbance. The rising must finally be here – but what are we to do in the town?

27th May (later)
News has just come that our forces have defeated the government troops at Oulart Hill. We would hardly believe it except that the news comes from soldiers from these same troops, and those fleeing from "the cursed rebels" as they put it.

Tom thinks we should join them and fight. Father

says we must wait. The arrests of the men who are supposed to be giving instructions and passing on orders from Dublin have left things in a confused state. For the moment, no one in the town seems to have declared themselves a United Irishman. We are all laying low.

Perhaps it is the wisest course of action for now, but I understand Tom's restlessness. It is difficult to do nothing when things are happening elsewhere.

28th May

We are still waiting. Every time Tom launches into one of his tirades about why can't we just raid the nearest loyalist house for arms (we have managed to hide our pikes but if we were to get our hands on pistols that would be even better), Father reminds him of how easy this town is to defend, with the walls all around us. "We might win out in the open, out on the hills," he has said more than once today, "but in the town, things would be very different."

29th May

More troops have arrived in the town – I think they are from Donegal.

There are loyalists seeking refuge here, believing the town to be safer than the countryside. They come with terrible tales of what the "rebels" are doing, but they must be exaggerations, surely. They are stories told to excuse what the loyalist forces – the yeomanry and the militia – are doing to the rebels, no doubt.

29th May (later)

They have just sent Fitzgerald and Colclough to Enniscorthy to talk to the rebels – they have been let out of prison to make this journey, in the hope of restoring the peace, I suppose.

"Fine lot of good talk will be now," is what John has to say on the matter.

"What happens if they do stand down?" I asked, meaning the rebels. Our people. "What will we do then?"

He shook his head. "I don't know. If they stand down now, we have no chance. We can't rise alone."

Mother is so tense she jumps whenever one of us comes near. She keeps muttering to herself. I think she is praying for us.

30th May

This morning there is a fire at the end of the bridge leading into town and worries from many of the loyalist townspeople about what it means.

Can this be it?

30th May

There are green flags everywhere – Irish flags! – and the town is swarming with those who have fought elsewhere as well as those of us who have finally joined them, free to announce ourselves now. Wexford is under our control, and we are celebrating. There are musicians on the streets, and green cockades to be seen on many hats.

Even Mother looks less anxious than usual. She has been distributing food to some of the new arrivals and listening to some of the stories about the battles and the camps. There have been losses, of course, but today we celebrate the gain – the town! I can hardly believe it. We are still waiting to hear news from Dublin but surely they must have had success too. It is happening!

31st May

The ships in the harbour that were meant to take loyalists away to safety have returned, manned by United Irishmen. Last night one of the passengers, a brother of the hateful James Boyd, tried to escape and earned himself a savage piking. Tom takes some of the credit for this. I am not sure whether to believe him or not. At any rate no one ran to help the man, just let him bleed, and eventually someone took a hatchet to him and put him out of his misery.

Despite this, the stories about the terrible things the rebels have been doing seem to be just that, stories. Some of the yeomen seem to have been afraid of what might happen, and are now out of uniform, but there have been no attacks made on them. Most of the troops have left. It is civilised.

We are gathering weapons, some of them reclaimed from the stash handed over to the magistrates not so long ago, some of them newly made or repaired.

We are waiting for what happens next.

11th July

I have been meaning to write for the last number of days but the words simply will not come.

It seems impossible that it has only been a few weeks since we set off from the town.

I am home now, with Mother, and we shuffle around the house like ghosts. This morning we sat together at breakfast and didn't say a word to each other.

The house has remained intact, more or less. For that I am grateful. And Mother is alive.

There are cottages and people throughout the county, including many of those just outside the town, that have not been so lucky.

13th July

They tell stories of what happened, and what is still happening. I know there are still some men out there fighting, hiding in the hills. There is still talk of the French coming. But it all seems so empty now. Empty promises.

The town is back in the hands of forces loyal to the Crown, and our dreams have been crushed.

I want to write down my stories before they become muddled with everyone else's accounts of what has happened. Before they are embellished or edited to suit one side or another. But already it is difficult to remember the precise order of things, and how it felt.

I know that once we were hopeful. We would have our own republic, we thought.

The day after the celebrations in the town, we gathered outside on one of the nearby hills and waited instructions. After much discussion one group was sent south. We were sent north, towards the camp at Vinegar Hill, just outside Enniscorthy, with a view to eventually taking Gorey. Our leaders included Anthony Perry, who was by then badly scarred – he had been tortured and pitchcapped during his arrest – but still going. He had a habit of screaming at the enemy during battles. It was as though he was getting all his anger out that way.

Who else was there at that stage? Some of them moved to other camps, or returned to the town, but I think two of the priests were there. One of them, Father John Murphy, had already made a name for himself by leading the rebels at Boolavogue and Oulart, even though he had originally been opposed to rebellion. One of the men I met told me of how the priest had preached to the congregation about handing over weapons, and then not a day later was urging them all to take up arms. It sounds too fantastical to be true, but it may well be. There were so many tales of shifting loyalties.

This is the thing. It is already so difficult to sift the truth from the lies.

14th July

The executions in the town have calmed down now. There are still some prisoners, and others who I think must be in hiding, not trusting that they will truly be pardoned. I understand that feeling all too well.

I missed the warmth of my bed, all the time I was out there. My first night home, my bed was the most extraordinary comfort of all. I shouldn't have taken any comfort in anything. I didn't deserve to. I still don't. But I can't help it. Should I sleep on the floor for the rest of my life as a penance? Perhaps.

Sometimes I feel I am indeed a coward, or worse. A traitor.

14th July (later)

Nine years ago on this day the French stormed the Bastille prison.

Seven years ago on this day in Belfast, celebrating that anniversary, the United Irishmen were formed.

Today there is little to celebrate.

The symbol of the United Irishmen, the harp with

the words, "It is new strung and shall be heard", is haunting me today.

It has been heard and then silenced.

Or perhaps – and this is what haunts me even more – it is being heard elsewhere in the country, and there will be another change of fortune, and I will be found to have abandoned the side of right.

Perhaps I should creep out of my bed late at night and make my way into the hills and join whatever forces I find. Or be shot by the redcoats, should they stumble across me. That seems more likely. And even if I did join the forces again, if they are still out there, would it be any use, now?

It would be braver not to have these doubts, perhaps. But I am not that brave.

15th July

Things began going badly for us on our approach to Gorey. We encountered the yeomanry and had to retreat long before we arrived at the town. For the next few days we stayed at the camp, practicing drills, which was tiresome but at least gave us something to do. It made me feel like more of a soldier and less of a boy not quite sure of what to do. The military experience of some of the leaders was comforting. We may not have worn uniforms but we were an army.

I think it was at that stage we began hearing of what had happened in the other counties. We learned that

Dublin was still under Castle control, that the rising was not the province or nation-wide success we had hoped. We were on our own.

I remember Father looking, for the first time, defeated when this news arrived. He had been almost cheerful as we marched, one of a number of the older professional men who made up our ranks. But then he began to seem worn out by it all. I think he had hoped it would be quicker.

I think we all hoped that. We hoped we would be part of something greater, with groups like ours all over the country ready to fight for a united, free Ireland.

Eventually we did move towards Gorey again, and after me sneaking around and exchanging fire and being utterly terrified, we took the town. So much of it is a blur. So much of it was marching, or waiting, or hiding. Even when we were winning, we were losing – by which I mean we lost men.

No. I don't mean lost. I mean they died. They were shot at. And we left them there.

15th July (later)
We left them there. On the ground.

I remember screaming. I remember not wanting to leave – no, more than that. I was unable to move.

I remember my father's body torn apart by musket fire.

I remember arms grabbing me and John's voice in my ear telling me we needed to move on.

I have no idea where his body is now. I know many of the troops did horrible things to the bodies they came across. Some were tossed in the rivers, others just left to rot.

Mother still hasn't asked me about Father. And I haven't said a word. She knows he is dead. But we don't talk about it.

There are so many things we don't talk about.

16th July

Most of what I remember from that time involves going out into the countryside with the others and gathering up two important resources – loyalist prisoners, who were kept in the market house in the town, and food. We took cattle from the nearby farms, and it kept us alive. It was curious how important food became. It took up so much of our time.

One of our leaders was a man named Edward Roche who made a grand proclamation to us all one day. This line I remember: "What power can resist men fighting for liberty?" It sounded so noble, so full of hope. Europe was watching, he said, and posterity would remember our heroic acts.

We felt like a part of history, even though we were ragged and stinking and dirty.

For a day, at least, I felt as though perhaps Father

had died for something worthy. I remember even saying this to John – we were drinking whiskey that had been stolen from a loyalist house, and I felt like a man, a man who was a part of things. "He died for the nation," I said, and John nodded and clapped me on the back, and we toasted him.

16th July (later)

Did we pitch-cap our prisoners? Yes.

I didn't. Not personally. Tom was involved, I know. He loved it. There was a curious way his face lit up whenever he exacted revenge, as he saw it.

"We should be better than that," John muttered, but there was no room for such thought then.

17th July

News comes of more rebels quashed by the mighty Crown forces. I feel ill. Even as there is order restored to our town, there is disruption elsewhere.

I am not a man. I am a small boy taking comfort and shelter from his mother, even though she barely says a word, still.

The world is grotesque. It feels full of shadows. Perhaps they have always been there and I never noticed them.

There has always been death, but what we have seen and heard of is the kind that belongs in stories, told around a fire, not in our lives.

I thought it was something that happened to other people. Old people, who had made their peace with God, or heroic figures who somehow knew it was a worthwhile sacrifice. I never realised it was something that could just happen, so quick, or so agonisingly slowly, and that so much of it could happen all at once.

There came a time in the hills when we moved towards Wicklow. I remember the approach to Arklow, the arguments along the way amongst the leaders and the ordinary men about whether or not to try to take the town, and if so how to go about it.

I remember the redcoats charging at us, and the thatched roofs of the nearby cottages going up in fire, and smoke everywhere, thick and confusing, beginning to choke us.

We were ordered to keep going, to keep trying. We would fall back and regroup and then try again. As the evening drew in and our ammunition began to run out, the general retreat to Gorey was ordered.

Some of the troops on horseback followed us as we tried to escape. I ran. I ran as fast as I could. My legs and chest ached and I could hardly breathe but I kept going. Our bodies are weaker than we like to admit to ourselves. I thought the fear would make me invincible, but instead I became conscious of just how vulnerable I was, how one shot would be the end of me.

We left men, dead or dying, in ditches, at the side of

the road, wherever they had fallen. I left them. This time, I knew that my brothers might be among them. I knew that there were men I had come to think of as friends who might have died, or worse might be dying, and screaming out for comfort, or a familiar face, or a priest to administer the last rites.

This time, I did not stop.

18th July

I should have nightmares. I should dream of suffocating smoke and spreading bloodstains and guts on the battlefield.

Instead my dreams are empty. Every night I sleep in my comfortable bed and I dream of nothing.

29th July

All the news is of United Irish executions. Henry Joy McCracken in Belfast, who led the too-brief Antrim rising that I only heard about after returning home. Perry and Father Kearns were found and executed in Offaly. There are others still being tried in Dublin.

Every single one feels like a heavy-handed lesson. This is what happens when you dare question the mighty power of Britain. I know that the men who make the decisions have something to prove. Both General Lake, who is in charge of the Crown forces throughout the country, and the Lord Lieutenant, Cornwallis, fought in the American war. Having lost their colonies there, they are not prepared to let our little island out of British control.

If only, if only, if only. If only we had had more ammunition. If only we had had better strategies. If only Dublin had had a successful rising, and the rest of the country had fallen in line. If only.

There is more I need to write about what happened out there, after the first attempt to take Arklow.

There were so many wounded. I realised too late I should not have run, but instead helped drag as many of the wounded as I could to safety. But I was tired, and scared, and others were running too. Is that any excuse?

We set up field hospitals, or rather put the wounded in any buildings in Gorey that seemed remotely suitable. I was bleeding from scratches and scrapes from the gorse but nothing as dreadful as these men and I knew not to complain. Some of the women in our camp tended to them, bandaging them up. We were glad of the civilians at times like that, the women and children who were usually there with a father or husband or brother, but sometimes just wanted to help. They helped supply our food, too. Sometimes I looked at the young children and hated them. I hated that there was no expectations of them, and that they had their mothers with them.

This is the truth: I wanted Mother there. It shames me even to admit that. I wanted someone to take care of me.

And I particularly wanted someone in those hours

when I thought I must be all alone in the world. There was no sign of Tom or John, and I knew we had lost many men. That word 'lost' again!

I was sure both my brothers were dead. And then later that day John threw his arms around me and I almost wept.

29th July (later)

It is painful to remember that moment before I knew Tom had died, and when I was so happy to see John again and to know he had survived.

He was the one who told me. "Robert," he began, but that was all that needed to be said. There was no one else important enough to us to merit such a sad expression across his face.

"Did you see it happen?" I wanted to know.

John shook his head. He'd been told by one of the other men.

"He was always going to get himself killed," I said suddenly. I didn't know then, and still don't, where those words came from. But I was furious with him for dying. "He didn't care about liberty or brotherhood or any of it. He was just looking for a fight."

"Don't say that."

"Why not? It's true." And I knew it was. Those newspapers and pamphlets and books with their fine ideas – Tom had never read them. Father had. John had. And after a time so had I.

John shook me then, roughly. "Don't get all high and mighty with me. Don't forget we took the oath long before you did, a mhuirnín!"

He had never sounded so like Tom as he did in that moment. For the next day we hardly said a word to each other.

The coldness between us passed, though. It had to. The following night, a few of us told stories of the men that had died, and I could feel John's hand grip my shoulder as if to remind me that we only had each other left.

I would give anything to feel that grip again.

31st July

I suppose it was still early June when we were told we were moving on Arklow again, this time to try to lure the troops out onto open ground rather than taking the town. The towns with their narrow streets were always troubling. We had more of a chance in the countryside, where we could move more freely. I remember being told this, and thinking about Father.

We waited. And waited.

We made camp in the mountains, moving from one hill to another. Eventually some of our number moved towards Tinahely, a small enough village but known for its loyalist activity.

We set it on fire.

When they saw the smoke, other groups from

Wicklow and Kildare joined us, and we learned more about what had happened in Dublin. How there must have been an informer, because they knew of the plan and crushed it before it even had a real chance to grow. We also heard that there were rumours of a French invasion any day now, and if we could just hold on then surely victory would be ours.

There was so much holding on. Just hold on. Just hold on. And here we are weeks later and there is still no sign of these French troops we placed so much faith in.

2nd August

I remember the leaders arguing about whether we should retreat further into the mountains and hide until the French arrived, or whether we should defend the borders of the county. We argued about it amongst ourselves too.

"We need to move towards Dublin," someone would say, and make a case for taking the capital. And then someone else would yell, "What about our families and homes? We need to protect them before we can even think about Dublin."

"If we return home and the king's troops have rallied, we're all dead men," someone else would contribute, and on and on it would go.

The feared General Lake's troops were moving in by this point. We would stay for now, it was decided.

We were so weary. That is the main thing I remember: the weariness.

The orders came to move to Vinegar Hill, where we would all gather instead of being in separate groups all over the county. It was already late at night when the word came, but we moved immediately.

The rain began shortly after. It hadn't rained for weeks, and it seemed like a bad omen. I said as much to John and he laughed and told me not to be superstitious. But I wasn't the only one who thought it meant something.

We were wet and tired and there was no chance to rest. Lake's men were close, we knew. We needed to keep moving. My legs felt like lead. It is like a dream now, or maybe a nightmare. If you asked me to retrace our steps I wouldn't be able to tell you. At one point I almost nodded off on my feet, and was jolted awake by the men on either side of me.

When we arrived at Vinegar Hill we slept, but it couldn't have been for long. A couple of hours, perhaps. It was still dark when we heard the boom of the cannon.

After that it was all chaos. Lake's men were better armed. They were better prepared. They shot at us and the civilians that were there, all of us jumbled together. There were explosive shells that they fired into the camp, killing several men at a time. It was like nothing else I have ever seen.

It truly was a nightmare.

We kept fighting. We did inflict some casualties on their side, I know. But it wasn't enough. We hoped for reinforcements from Wexford town that never came. I later discovered the town had its own problems at that time, with so-called 'trials' of the loyalist prisoners leading to almost a hundred of them being massacred on the bridge. We knew nothing of that then, though.

We had to retreat. Those of us that could.

I was covered with the blood of men who had died from those shells, and barely able to breathe. I knew I was alive. And I knew this was the end of it.

If we had won the battle, things would have been very different. That was the hope – to unite all the Wexford forces for a great victory. Instead John and I began to make our way back home.

Some might call it desertion. Some of the men were determined to stay and fight no matter what, and they broke into smaller groups and went their separate ways. Some of them are likely still out there, though I would wager not that many. But John and I were not the only ones to slip away that day.

Was this an act of cowardice? It often feels like it.

There was so much death that day. It was unthinkable.

We did not go straight home, but instead went to Jenny's family, outside the town. She hardly recognised us when we first approached her. We were so filthy and ragged, like beggars. If I had been more myself I would have felt ashamed, but we were simply so grateful for the resting place. It was safe there.

My hand grows tired – I will finish tomorrow. It needs to be written.

3rd August

Jenny's family had been largely left alone during the weeks of bloodshed. Those in the town knew they were decent folk. Her father had the reputation of supporting Catholics, and I suppose people may have known his nephews were United Irishmen.

She did tell us about a group carrying out forced conversions, with the help of one of the local priests. She and a number of other Protestants had been dragged outside to be baptised and to renounce their old faith.

"The priest told me just to nod," she said. "I don't think he wanted to be there at all, but the rebels were so insistent that we needed to convert to Catholicism."

John was furious. "That should never have happened. How dare these men call themselves United Irishmen and then partake in – in – a religious war!"

It was astonishing he was able to be furious about that after all we had seen. Because if I am honest, it did not sound like such a terrible thing. Not in comparison to all the death we had seen, or the screams of women and children we had heard.

The truth is that while we were not fighting a religious war, it seems clear that some of our forces were. Mother was right. Some of them had no interest in the ideals of the United Irishmen, for us to build a nation where men of all beliefs could come together and govern in a reasonable manner. Some of the Catholics just wanted revenge on Protestants for old grievances, and any Protestant would do.

When our forces reached New Ross, and lost the battle there, they burned their prisoners alive in retaliation. There was perhaps a hundred of them, Protestant men, women and children, all locked in a barn at Scullabogue. If I had been there – if I had been part of that group that went south instead of north the day after we took control of Wexford town – perhaps I might have said something. Said, "Stop, we will show mercy, we are better than they are." Or I might have asked, "Why are we doing this – just because they are Protestants? This is not what we swore to. This is not what we wanted."

In my head I make magnificent speeches that persuade the others that we are nobler and better than that.

I know it is a lie. I know that the words would have fallen on deaf ears. There was no place for sentiment when we were fighting.

We were ragged and tired and hungry. We must have had an awful stench but after a while it became hardly noticeable. It is astonishing how quickly you get used to things.

It is easy to think now that I might have spoken up. I wouldn't have. Not then. Not in that moment.

But there was no need for it. No need for any of it.

3rd August (later)

We heard of General Lake's proclamation that rebels who surrendered would be granted clemency.

"Turn yourself in," Jenny urged us both. She looked at John with such tenderness in her eyes that it was clear she did love him.

I think Father was wrong. She would have married him, if they had been given the chance, no matter what her family thought of it.

"How can we be sure they won't just hang us?" John said.

"If you're found here, you will be hanged," she said. "But if you show your remorse now, and show that you're ready to be loyal again . . ."

She seemed so hopeful that all would be well. For her, General Lake was restoring order. I know from what John had said that she was sympathetic to the cause, but even her limited encounters with the rebels seemed to have persuaded her that peace was worth any price.

When we finally agreed to take advantage of the amnesty, John had been infected by Jenny's optimism.

I, on the other hand, was numb. It felt as though we were walking through fog.

I remembered then – I can still see it so clearly even now – how, in the beginning, we were disgusted at those who had handed over their weapons and sworn allegiance to the king.

"We'll die first," Tom said.

And the three of us nodded fiercely.

Then there was just the two of us and Tom had indeed died before surrendering and all I could do was put one foot in front of the other over and over again.

I don't remember much of it. Or perhaps I don't want to. Perhaps my mind knows it is too painful to think about.

They granted me a pardon, looking at me with pity as if to say, 'How did you get caught up in all this?' My child-like face and scrawny stature saved me. I couldn't possibly be any harm to them in the future. I wasn't impressive enough to be made an example of.

They made an example out of John instead.

5th August

So many of them were hanged on the bridge. Not just John, but the leaders like Keogh and Father Roche and Harvey.

Here is what I remember: they cut Keogh's head off and stuck it on a pike and paraded it around the streets like a trophy. They did the same for Harvey a few days later.

They had to hang Father Roche twice because the rope snapped. It was awful.

John was brave. Braver than I would have been. He did not weep. He was white as a sheet but he said nothing. And then they hanged him just like the rest of them and he was gone – all the life vanished from his face.

I should have persuaded him not to trust that we would be treated fairly. I should have thought more clearly about it. How on earth could we have believed that the men who had slaughtered so many of our kind were now ready to be entirely forgiving?

I went home with my pardon and Mother, with red eyes, didn't need to ask what had happened to the rest of our family.

I should tell her. It has been weeks now, and the pain has dulled slightly – yet still I sometimes wake up and think I am back at the camp, and I look for Father or John or Tom. And then I remember. I remember the awful truth.

They are dead.

There are so many dead. And it has all come to nothing.

Would it be easier to have lost them if we had gained a republic? Would I sacrifice them for that grand noble ideal?

It is difficult to imagine I ever thought in such terms.

25th August

The French have arrived in Mayo.

I heard the news and wept bitterly.

What good will it do now?

27th September

In weaker moments over the last few weeks I have imagined what might happen if the French forces in Connaught defeated General Lake's troops. I have imagined a re-emergence of the United Irishmen here and throughout the country. In these visions somehow Father is alive again, and I stand between my two brothers, and it is all noble and glorious instead of grubby and bloody and painful.

It is all irrelevant. The French have been defeated, just as we were.

12th November

Wolfe Tone, who turned out to be one of the 'French officers' that landed at Lough Swilly in County Donegal earlier this month, has been captured. Major Holt, the last great United Irish leader, has surrendered. This is the end of it. I know there are men in the town, United Irishmen who have managed to stay alive through pardons or chance, who have held out hope until now.

For me it is just another reminder that hope died a long time ago.

Dublin, 1800

June 21ˢᵗ

It has been two years since that terrible final battle at Vinegar Hill.

This year, as I did last year, I choose this date to remember Father and Tom and John, because it is the one date I can safely link to a particular event, even if it is not a date any of them died upon. The rest of the days all blur together.

The Rising has become a story that is told, over and over, the way all stories are. I am glad to have written down my version of events. There are times when the memories and the stories seem to merge, and I momentarily forget, for example, whether I was actually at Scullabogue, where all those terrible things happened, or if it was only a tale told to me after the fact.

There are others writing and telling their versions, and I cannot say if all those who were part of the king's troops will lie or exaggerate to make us seem more monstrous than we were, but I suspect it. We were no worse than they were, which is no excuse, of course.

And now the government are passing Acts of Union to make Ireland part of England. The parliament will be gone from Dublin, and instead of being ruled by those loyal to England we will instead be ruled by England. How this was ever agreed to I can't imagine.

No. I know how it was agreed to. It seems to those fools in parliament like a way to ensure that a rising can never happen again. And there has been bribery and corruption too – we all know it, not that it does any of us any good. There are some of us in the city that are furious, but what are we to do with this anger? At times I miss having weapons to hand, I will admit, but then I remember that for all the weapons I carried over those weeks in '98 I am not sure I ever managed to strike a fatal blow, not once.

There is still blood on my hands, though, on all our hands. But there is far more on theirs. I cannot imagine this Union will bring about peace. If anything it seems like it is guaranteed to bring about rebellion.

I am not sure I am ready to fight again. I am not a soldier. But I hope I live to see it, when it comes. Because it *will* come – it must. Perhaps that is what the stories of the Rising will be for – to make sure that day does come, when Ireland is finally free.

I will keep telling my story, which is this: my father and my brothers and I fought for what we believed in. A free Ireland. A better Ireland. A brighter future.

If I close my eyes now I can almost see it.

Afterword

While the main characters in these stories (and their families and friends) are invented, the events and the political figures mentioned are real. The eighteenth century was an Age of Enlightenment, a time when many new ideas were circulating on both sides of the Atlantic and when older ideas were being criticised. The traditional power structures – like kings or other privileged people being in charge even though they hadn't been elected – began to seem unfair, but they were also what people were used to.

When the American colonists rebelled against the British, it was hugely inspiring. Even though it was a costly war, the colonies gained their independence and began their 'experiment in democracy' – one which is still going strong! The revolutionary ideals spread to France, eventually leading to the creation of a republic and a sense of a new beginning so strong that a new calendar was invented. Again the cost was high – the threats to the new republic from all sides led to the horrors of the Terror, and the republic couldn't last.

It did, however, last long enough to inspire the United Irishmen to begin thinking about, and working towards, a republic of their own. The rising of 1798 ended in defeat, but in the years that followed, people told stories of the Rising and wrote many songs to remember the bravery of the men who fought for freedom – and to keep the spirit of '98 alive.

These must have been difficult – though often exciting – times to live through. These were violent uprisings – but these were people living in violent times, and they didn't have very many options available to them if they wanted to stand up for themselves. It's difficult to imagine now what that might have been like, but stories can help us try . . .

Another way we can try to imagine what it was like in the eighteenth century is to read newspapers and other documents from that time. If you're interested in this, there are some great resources available online which relate to the topics covered in this book:

The Massachusetts Historical Society: The Coming of the American Revolution 1764-1776 – http://masshist.org/revolution/index.html

Liberty, Equality, Fraternity: Exploring the French Revolution – http://chnm.gmu.edu/revolution/

National Archives of Ireland: The Rebellion of 1798 – http://www.nationalarchives.ie/PDF/1798.pdf

Also in the HANDS ON HISTORY *Series*

The Easter Rising 1916 - *Molly's Diary*

Easter 1916. The Great War rages in Europe with two hundred thousand Irishmen fighting in the British Army. But a small group of Irish nationalists refuse to fight for Britain and strike a blow for Irish Freedom. Caught up in the action in Dublin is twelve-year-old Molly O'Donovan.

Her own family is plunged into danger on both sides of conflict. Her father, a technical officer with the Post Office, dodges the crossfire as he tries to restore the telegraph lines, while her wayword brother runs messages for the rebels. Molly, a trained First Aider, risks her own safety to help the wounded on both sides.

As violence and looting erupts in the streets of Dublin alongside heroism and high ideals, Molly records it all. The Proclamation at the GPO, the arrival of the British troops, the Battle of Mount Street.

But will Molly's own family survive and will she be able to save her brother? This is her diary.

ISBN 978-178199-9745

Acknowledgements

Many thank-yous! Bear with me, gentle reader.

Thanks to everyone at Poolbeg Press, particularly Paula Campbell for letting me play in this historical sandbox, and Gaye Shortland for her thoughtful editing.

Thank you to Sallyanne Sweeney at Mulcahy Associates for her assistance and wisdom in matters both businessy and writerly.

I am very, very grateful to Eimear Ryan, Fiona Deverell, Jenny Duffy, Colm McDonagh and Carol McGill for reading drafts of different bits of this story and for their insights.

Many thanks to my friends for their support and general fabulousness, in particular Eimear Ryan (yes, again, the woman deserves a medal), Laura Cassidy, Deirdre Sullivan, and Andrea Wickham. (The rest of ye are marvellous too, obviously. I owe ye many hugs.)

I wouldn't have dreamed of dipping my toes into the days of yore were it not for some very excellent history teachers – Sarah O'Neill at Loreto Beaufort, and Joseph Clarke and David Dickson at Trinity College Dublin.

Finally – thank you, dear reader! I very much hope you enjoy the book.